DANGEROUS KING

SIENNA SNOW

D1604393

Dangerous King

Copyright © 2021 by Sienna Snow

Published by Sienna Snow

HELLO LOVELY BOX LIMITED EDITION 2023

www.siennasnow.com

Hello Lovely Box Limited Edition 2023 Cover Design: Kat Savage

Hello Lovely Box Limited Edition 2023 Interior Formatting: Persephone Autumn | Between Words Publishing LLC

ISBN - eBook - 978-1-948756-21-1

ISBN - Print - 978-1-948756-22-8

♡ Sienna Shaw

CHAPTER ONE

DANIKA

"Why bother showing up if you were going to frown all night?" I muttered to my cousin Jayna as she glared at her father, my Uncle Ashok, for the fifth time in less than ten minutes.

We stood to one side of the massive ballroom of the Andhi New York City, one of the many boutique hotels under the conglomerate my uncle owned.

Tonight's gala had everyone from the upper crust of Manhattan society to A-list celebrities in attendance. They were here more to rub elbows with each other, to be seen, or to make the next deal than to support the charity the event championed.

I, on the other hand, had to be here. Given the choice, I'd rather be head deep in a pile of paperwork for the gallery I ran with Jayna than pretending to enjoy the socialite lifestyle. Sometimes I wished I were more like Jayna. She had always marched to the beat of her own drum. If Uncle Ashok had ordered her to attend any event, she'd have ignored him and done what she'd wanted. Nothing seemed to scare her, least of all the wrath of her father. But then again, we weren't all born into the circumstances she was.

"Some of us aren't lap dogs like you, who jump whenever he calls."

Direct hit.

I resisted clenching my jaw and tried to hide the pain I felt every time anyone referred to me as Ashok Shah's lap dog.

It was my own fault. I'd become indispensable to Uncle Ashok, making it so he would never question my loyalty to him.

Ever.

If he needed me to research something or make some connection, I'd do it. If he needed a date for an event or for me to represent him at a fundraiser, I'd do it.

I played the dutiful niece who he'd plucked from poverty and placed into a life of opulence and luxury. The one who let the world believe I was the perfectly molded, well-educated society princess.

If only people knew the truth.

I lived in a gilded cage.

One partly of my own making. But for a good cause. And for a multitude of reasons. Reasons that ran as deep as razors to the core of my soul.

Truth be told, I hated Uncle Ashok with every fiber of my being. And one day, I planned to dismantle his empire brick by brick.

Patience was the key to achieve my goal, and I was slowly setting up each piece of the puzzle. Until that day, I'd let others believe what they wanted about me, no matter how much it hurt to hear.

Well, it pissed me off when Jayna made her comments.

She knew me better than most people; she should know the truth.

"Haven't you ever heard of the saying 'keep your friends close but your enemies closer'?"

"That doesn't mean that you jump every time he says so."

"That's exactly what it means. It's part of the game, Jay. If he thinks I'm loyal to the bone, he won't look in my direction when things don't go his way."

"I want him to suffer, Dani." Jayna pursed her lips again. "He's taken too much from us."

"He will. I promise."

I glanced to my side and studied Uncle Ashok as he mingled with the event attendees. A beautiful blonde stood next to him—Amber Tuttle, a former property developer and widow of one of my uncle's investors.

They made a striking couple in their late fifties. It was obvious they took care of themselves.

Every interaction I had with Amber told me she was a kind person with an innocent heart. She believed Uncle was the illusion of the man he'd created, instead of the monster I'd grown up with. She wanted to become the next Mrs. Shah. Poor woman had no idea she was in for a surprise if it ever happened.

Hopefully, Amber would do her due diligence before jumping in. She had a fortune and her sanity on the line.

The one woman she should consult before making any life decisions was Auntie Monica, Uncle Ashok's ex-wife. She suffered for twenty-five years under Uncle's hand. That was until she built the courage needed to leave.

The women in this house lack discipline. If only God saw fit to give me someone in this house worthy of the Shah name.

Jayna and I had lived through enough of his form of

discipline to know he believed the women in his life were to do as he said or suffer the consequences.

"What aren't you telling me?" Jayna probed, snapping me back to the present.

"A lot. It's better you stay in the dark."

I couldn't reveal anything yet. I had to have irrefutable proof of Uncle Ashok's corruption. Plus, the moment I let my plan hit the air, it would no longer be a secret. The fewer people who knew, the better.

"As I told you when I decided to come tonight, I don't need you to play interference between me and Papa anymore. It's time for me to take my life back."

"Meaning?" I asked as I smiled at a New York City councilwoman and her husband as they passed us.

"Exactly what I said. I lost Kiran, but that doesn't mean my life ended when his did. And what better way to gain some semblance of normal back than by destroying the bastard that took my love from me. Please, let me help."

I stared at Jayna for a second. There was no way I could hide my surprise at the way she spoke so casually about Kiran's death.

For the last few years, I could barely mention my childhood friend's name without worry about hurting Jayna. Kiran had been killed in an explosive car crash almost two years ago, where nothing had remained of his body but bits of bone and ash. The trauma of her loss followed by a mugging that resulted in a miscarriage had her becoming all but a recluse.

The only times she ventured out of her townhouse were to work at the clubs and the art gallery she owned or to help me with some projects for my exclusive clients. Over the last four months, she'd done neither, spending most of her time on a private island off the coast of Greece owned by Sylvia Thanos. A woman we affectionately called *Yia Yia* Sylvia.

She was the grandmother of one of my girlfriends and a very good client, who happened to be an eccentric billionaire who had her hands in everything, legal and illegal. Sylvia had a tendency of taking in lost souls, healing them, and then sending them out into the world again. And it seemed as if Sylvia had worked her magic on Jayna.

"Jay, I'm not sure."

"Come on. I need to feel like myself again."

I examined her face. She looked so much healthier than when she'd left. The shadows under her eyes that I thought would become permanent had faded and she'd finally gained enough weight to return to her curvy bombshell figure. I'd felt guilty for pushing a reluctant Jayna to take Sylvia's offer of an extended vacation and now I was glad I had. Her whole energy was different.

Maybe I could convince Sylvia to work her magic on me when I finally took that long- overdue vacation I kept promising myself.

For now, I had to keep my focus and keep my eyes on the goal.

The fall of Ashok Shah.

"If you're serious about helping me, then I'll bring you in, but it will be on my time, not yours."

She pursed her lips in annoyance. "You're really not going to tell me what you're up to?"

"Let me get a few more things in order and I'll share everything. Uncle Ashok is setting the stage for something and I want the details before I execute my plan."

"Who are you and what did you do with my cousin?" Jayna grabbed two wine flutes from a passing server, handing me one and downing the other before I'd barely grabbed hold of my stem. "I'm the rebel, not you."

Jayna being the rebel was an understatement. She'd mastered the ability to bring Uncle Ashok to the point of killing rage with just a look.

"You've been in Europe for the last four months. A lot has happened. You have your way of getting back at Uncle, and I have my way."

What would she do if she knew I'd spent the last ten years of my life setting the stage for this? No. I could never let her know. Those were my secrets.

"Give me an example."

I thought for a second and decided to tell her of the latest debacle in Uncle Ashok's world. I was quite proud of it, and no one would ever know I was behind the leak.

"I may have let it slip to certain parties that Uncle was buying a property for his expansion project."

"Are you talking about the waterfront project? The one the news is reporting that unless the rezoning goes through, Papa can't build the new hotel and shopping complex?"

I gave a sheepish smile and said, "Maybe."

The project was supposed to be the proverbial cherry on top of Uncle's empire. An empire built on the backs of more innocent people than anyone would ever know. I'd never regret fucking with his plans.

"That would mean you contacted Nik. Since when are you and Nik on speaking terms?"

The mention of Nikhil King's name had my heartbeat speeding up and every nerve in my body firing.

He was the forbidden fruit. The man who I couldn't have. The link to my past. A past I could never forget and had to pretend never existed. And the one person who'd always played center stage in every one of my fantasies.

"We aren't. I just happened to place an untraceable folder on his computer's desktop, giving him details on available properties for a youth center and museum."

"You hacked Nik?" Jayna shook her head. "Have you lost your ever-loving mind?"

I shrugged my shoulders. "Sanity is subjective, especially considering half of our genetic makeup and the hidden line of work I'm in."

"Damn, girl, you have some serious balls. I swear if they think it was me, I'll never hear the end of it."

"Yeah, right. You're smart, but you and I both know I'm the hacker extraordinaire out of our duo."

"This isn't a joke, Dani. Nik can't get even a small whiff of who hacked him. And then there's Sam and Rey. God, I think I'm going to get an ulcer. Dammit, they're going to think I put you up to this, if they ever find out." She pressed a hand to her stomach.

"You're so dramatic. When they try to trace the person who hacked them, it will lead them into a continuous loop to servers all over the world."

"I'm so glad you never told me about this before tonight. I would have tried to stop you."

"And hence the reason you just found out."

"Aren't you even a little worried?"

"No."

"Dani," she said in an exasperated tone. "Sooner or later, they'll find out. They always do."

"We'll cross that bridge if it happens."

I probably should never let her know that this wasn't the first time I'd put some information on one of the King brothers' computers.

"Are you even listening to me? They aren't sweet, lovable, understanding teddy bears. Hell, they're the exact opposite."

She acted as if I wasn't the one who grew up with them. I knew them better than she did.

The Kings lived on the edge of polite society. They had their hands in everything and were rumored to have ties to the unsavory elements of the world, which I knew was fact. They presented themselves as real estate developers with more money than Midas. But I'd known them before they were the Kings, when they had individual names and ran the streets of the neighborhood I'd lived in as a child. When they'd been my friends, the boys who'd protected the awkward, nerdy girl who never quite fit in.

"Calm down. It's not like I haven't done things like this before. Hell, I get paid big bucks to hack the most impenetrable of systems."

"Yes, but you weren't hired to hack the King brothers."

"That's true. Though my usual clients are billion-dollar companies, royal houses, and various government organizations." My answer garnered a glare from Jayna. Sighing, I set a hand on her forearm. "Jay, no one will believe Danika Dayal would have the knowledge to hack anything. I'm an art appraiser who helps you run your gallery and your father's lackey. I'm the poor relation, taken in to keep from destitution."

"Poor relation, my ass. You have more money than all of us."

"Well, no one knows this."

Over the course of the last nine years, I'd amassed a significant net worth from various jobs I'd undertaken. All of it hidden in Swiss accounts. I could technically afford to live a jet- setting life if I wanted to, but then again, I'd have to justify my newfound fortune. Something I wasn't going to let anyone outside of my inner circle know anything about.

"Let me repeat: the King brothers aren't just anyone. They find out things that people don't want to hit the light of day and use it to their advantage."

"Jay, it's not a big deal. I promise. Stop worrying. You wanted an example of how I wasn't Uncle's lapdog and I gave it. Think of it this way: every time something goes wrong in his life, you can grin and think Dani may have had a hand in it."

"This is a dangerous game you're playing."

"I know." My voice grew serious. "Do you trust me?"

"Yes," she answered without hesitation.

"Then, trust that I know what I'm doing. I'm not as weak as I let everyone believe, even you. There are reasons why I'm doing things the way I am. When I have all the pieces lined up, there's going to be a lot of truth tea spilled. Tea that Uncle is going to drown in."

"And Nik is part of the plan?"

"He's…" I trailed off as my gaze locked on the very man.

He stood in the hallway outside of the ballroom with a phone to his ear. His dark, penetrating gaze studied me in a way I should have been used to by now, but always felt as if it was the first time. Everything inside me clenched in response.

Fuck.

He was gorgeous in the way that gave a woman heart palpitations, and no woman around him was immune.

Those broad shoulders and muscled arms gave truth to the rumors he spent more time than not in the boxing ring and probably meant there wasn't an ounce of unnecessary fat on his body. Then there were those piercing almost-black eyes that seemed to see too much with a simple look. And finally, his face looked as if it had been created by the discerning eye of a sculptor's chisel, but was the result of the beautiful union between his Afro-Trinidadian mother and Indian father.

The one thing that kept him from looking too perfect was the dusting of a beard, which only added to the unrefined edge he carried naturally. His whole aura made a woman think of all the wickedly delicious things he could do to her body.

I couldn't help but wonder what it would be like to run my fingers across his jaw just once. Or to kiss those lips I'd dreamed about over too many restless nights.

Nope, dammit, Danika. Don't go there. Put him back in that box of impossibilities. Well, at least for a little longer.

Maybe one day I could allow myself a taste, or if I was lucky, a night to indulge.

"What are you looking at? Oh." Jayna nudged me, snapping my attention back to her. "Are you sure you don't want Nik to be a bigger part of your plan than these games from afar?"

I swallowed, pushing down my thought from moments earlier, and said, "He's a complication I can't afford right now."

CHAPTER TWO

NIK

I inhaled deep, trying to control my body's reaction from the moment Danika Dayal's gaze landed on me.

I'd watched the gorgeous brunette socializing with New York City's elite as if she were born into it for the better part of the evening.

But I knew the truth.

She was a very good actress though, a chameleon, a woman who'd learned the hard way to navigate this new path and use it to her advantage. She played the game better than those born into it. All the while hiding the cunning intelligence underneath. A genius that had come to her naturally, something that wasn't cultivated in her new life but cast in the poverty-stricken neighborhood where we'd met.

She'd shed the taint of the dark streets and created a new life, whereas I used it to my advantage and wore it like a well-worn-in suit.

The one thing that had never changed in all the years was the way she looked at me.

It wouldn't matter if I was wearing a tux or a beat-up hoodie, heat would fill her hazel eyes for a few seconds before she schooled it away. It was a pattern we repeated over and over for too many years to count.

There was no doubt Shah had warned her away from anything and everything associated with the old neighborhood, especially me.

Shah had to have known what she meant to me when he'd taken her.

And for her sake, I'd stayed away. It had all but killed me. But what could a seventeen- year-old street kid with one foot away from jail or the grave give a brilliant girl who deserved so much more than the neighborhood she should never have stepped foot into in the first place?

Soon. Very soon. The waiting would be over. There was no doubt, and from the need staring at me, she knew it too.

Danika shifted her attention away as Jayna said something and then a group of people approached them.

"She's off-limits, Nik. Don't forget it," my brother Kiran warned through my phone, drawing my attention back to him while I kept my gaze on the goddess.

"Getting threats from a dead man isn't going to change something that was set in motion fifteen years ago. Besides, aren't you the one who said I had to make an appearance tonight? If it wasn't for you, I'd have stayed home and played poker with our crew."

I took a glass of champagne from a passing server. The last thing I wanted to do was attend an event at any of the Andhi properties. Ashok Shah, who'd taken more from my brothers and me than anyone would ever know. Making an appearance at an event in his honor felt like wading through a pile of shit.

According to Kiran, an appearance at this gala would throw Shah off-kilter. Especially since I held information that could put a spotlight on some of his behind-the-scenes business dealings. And keeping Shah on his toes was a sadistic pleasure I couldn't resist.

"If you fuck this up, you're the one who's going to be a dead man," Kiran warned.

"No, I'm just letting a plan older than yours work its way to the forefront." I downed the drink and set the flute on a nearby table.

"Six more months shouldn't make a difference."

"Danika's the key to everything. You know it as much as I do."

"And what about my wife? Have you thought about her safety?"

The corners of my lips lifted and I shook my head. Jayna looked as if she'd rather be anywhere but here. She never tried to hide her dislike of her father. This was her first formal appearance at one of his events in years.

Seeing her walk in with Danika had been an unexpected surprise. As far as I'd known, she wasn't due back in the States for another few weeks.

I planned to stop by her place tomorrow and have a discussion about keeping us informed of her whereabouts. She'd probably tell me to fuck off since she was as stubborn as her cousin, but it was my duty to keep her safe.

"She's stronger than you think, Kir. In fact, I'm staring at her right now."

Overall, she looked better than she had in a long time, and makeup made her look flawless, but there was still an air of sadness hidden underneath the elegant trappings. As far as she and the world knew, Kiran had died in a car crash.

One orchestrated by her father, Ashok Shah.

Shah believed his word was law, and anyone who didn't fall into line would suffer the consequences. Deep pockets could cover up the greatest of crimes.

What the bastard hadn't yet realized was that some of us had more than he could ever dream of achieving.

"What the hell is she doing there? She's supposed to be in Greece."

"How the fuck would I know? She's your wife."

"Dammit, she knows better. Is her security there?"

I scanned the area and found three of my men who worked as Jayna's personal protection scattered around the ballroom.

"Yes, she's not stupid," I responded, before asking, "Are you sure you don't want to tell her the truth?"

"No. I'm not ready for her to see me like this."

Kiran's crash had left him with scars on his face and along the left side of his back. Of my three brothers, Kiran had been known for his striking good looks. His unique Indian and Puerto Rican genetics had given him a baby face we'd loved to tease him about when we were kids. Now I'd love to go back to those days instead of having to keep every reflective surface away from him for fear of him breaking it.

"She gave up a giant inheritance to be with you. Have faith in her. She loves you. If she didn't, she'd have moved on by now."

Outside of her art gallery and the nightclubs she'd started as a fuck-you to her father, she had no life.

Not once in the nearly two years since Kiran's accident had she dated anyone.

"How does she look?" The longing in his voice whenever he spoke about her always hit me in the gut.

The tough-as-nails street kid who'd helped me run our scams to survive had fallen for the pampered princess harder than anyone could ever have imagined.

I just couldn't understand what made him believe his girl wouldn't be able to look at him without flinching.

"Good."

It was a half-truth but something that was necessary. I couldn't tell him that Jayna had lost the spark of joy that used to follow her whenever she entered a room.

Then I decided to add, "She'd look even better if you stopped hiding and trusted her."

"Let it go, asshole. Focus on the reason you're there."

"I am." My gaze went back to Danika. "Believe me, I am."

"Nik, I mean it. Don't use Dani to get to her uncle. She hates him as much as we do."

Something told me her hatred for Ashok was ten times deeper than any of us knew.

"The plan isn't for us to use her. The plan is for us to protect her. She is the one person who could bring down his empire."

"I have a feeling whatever you've cooked up is going to piss me off."

Ignoring Kiran, I said, "Shah wants what we have on him and he is going to use her to get it."

Shah lorded his control over his family and especially the niece he'd snatched from the streets.

"What makes you so sure?"

"I've never hidden that I wanted Danika. I have a feeling he's going to offer her in exchange for his mother's will. It's the only thing standing in the way of his plans for his future."

"I will kick your ass if you go through with it."

"For you to kick anyone's ass, you'd have to leave that cave you locked yourself in. Does Jayna know what a pussy she married?"

"Fuck off." Kiran hung up.

I slid my phone into my pocket and made my way into the ballroom.

I probably shouldn't have said the last part, but I'd let Kiran wallow for too long.

In the beginning, he was barely holding on to life. Then it was the excruciating physical rehab he'd had to survive. Now, he was just hiding, not only from Ashok, which he had to do, but from his wife. A person he should know would accept him in any form.

I pushed the thoughts of my brother back and watched the goddess across the ballroom.

Danika glanced in my direction for a brief second.

She was the opposite of the barely teen girl I'd known. The innocent who sat on the steps of her neighbor's corner shop so she wouldn't have to spend all day alone while her father worked. Gone were the simple jeans, T-shirt, and sneakers. Now she wore designer from head to toe.

The one thing that hadn't changed was the undeniable intelligence behind her eyes. Even back in the day, she was the smartest kid on the street.

I'd never understood why she'd followed me around when someone like her should have stayed far away from the street gang leader I'd been.

I couldn't count the number of times she'd covered for me and my brothers when the cops had combed our neighborhood for a group of kids who'd fleeced lost tourists out of wallets. And because she was known as the good girl, the cops believed her every time.

Then one day, she'd disappeared as if she'd never existed. On the very day one mistake had changed the path of my and my brothers' lives.

Now here Danika and I were, fifteen years later, playing a game where we were always aware of the other's presence without outwardly acknowledging it.

It was safe.

For her.

And in the beginning for me.

After her father's murder, Shah had made it his mission to scrub Danika's past from existence, her father, her mother, and especially me.

I'd kept an eye on her from a distance, letting her carve out a life beyond anything she could have dreamed of as a child.

It had worked until a chance encounter between Kiran and Jayna changed everything. Their relationship had forced Danika to become the shield between Shah and his daughter.

When Kiran and Jayna eloped, Shah clamped onto Danika, going as far as having her followed at all times to keep her from making the same mistakes his daughter and his sister had made.

I nodded a greeting to a banker who owed me a favor and then shifted my attention to Danika again. She was talking to Ashok Shah. Her face was emotionless but her eyes blazed with anger. After a curt nod, Ashok walked away and Danika moved toward a city councilman who was up for reelection. The practiced smile was back on her face.

What I wouldn't give to watch her use the self-defense moves I'd taught her as a kid to punch Ashok in the face.

Where the hell was Jayna? Was Danika playing interference again? I searched the room and found her standing in front of me.

"Are my eyes deceiving me, or is Nikhil King at an event in honor of Ashok Shah?"

"Is it really in his honor if he's the one throwing the party?"

She shook her head and then hugged me. "What are you doing here, Nik?"

"I could ask the same of you. Weren't you supposed to be in Greece for a few more weeks?"

"It was time to come back."

There was something different about her tonight. As if her energy was lighter.

God, I hoped she hadn't decided to move on. It would kill Kiran and finish what the crash hadn't.

"You look good. We missed you. But this isn't where I ever expected to see you. Didn't you say it would take an act of God to get you in the same room as your father?"

"He's not my father. DNA makes him a sperm donor, nothing more." "Then why are you here?"

"Because I realized Dani was taking the consequences of my choices and I was letting her. It wasn't fair to her, even if it was the easier choice for me. It was time to lighten the load on her plate."

Immediately, the protective urge I'd always had when it came to Danika surged forward. "What are you talking about? What is the bastard doing to her?"

Jayna set a hand on my arm. "Calm down—it's nothing more than we already know. I just accepted she has spent the last three years letting Papa think he's controlling her for my sake. It was time to let Dani have a life without restrictions."

Danika and Jayna were close as sisters; they were each other's closest confidants. Including keeping each other's darkest secrets. After Kiran's crash, Danika had grown even more protective of Jayna.

The relief I felt was short-lived as I caught on to the middle part of Jayna's words.

"What do you mean, he *thinks* he's controlling her?"

Jayna smiled, the first genuine smile I'd seen on her face in a long time. "Dani isn't as weak as Papa assumes. Hell, I've even underestimated her. She's playing him."

18

"How is that?"

"Those are things for me to know and you to only hope to find out."

"You're such a brat."

"Yep. That's never going to change." She slid her arm through mine and said, "Want to help me continue my brattiness and give me a hand in escaping this farce of a party?"

"What happened to not hiding behind your cousin?"

I looked across the ballroom at Danika. She watched me with as much intensity as I'd studied her earlier. Her eyes darted to Jayna and then to the door before returning to me. Then she motioned with her chin.

"I'm not. I said to that asshole's face I was leaving with you. Dani is talking to a client or I'd drag her with us."

"I doubt she'll ruin her pristine reputation by going anywhere in public with me."

Jayna smirked. "Don't judge a book by the fancy cover, Nik. She may surprise you. The girl has more secrets than you do."

"I seriously doubt that," I responded, and led Jayna toward the doors leading out of the ballroom.

CHAPTER THREE

DANIKA

Saturday evening, after a successful but long afternoon of private showings in the gallery, I walked into my apartment ready to binge-watch the new season of my favorite K-drama curled up on my couch with a bottle of wine.

Just as I kicked off my shoes and dropped my day bag on the front entrance table, my cellphone rang.

"Hello," I answered.

"I have a question for you," a polished feminine voice said.

I inhaled deep, knowing my plans for the evening were about to get shot to hell.

"Go ahead."

"Are you up for a game of poker?"

"Always," I said with a sigh and then added, "How much do I need to spend and what information do you need me to get?"

I moved into my living room and dropped onto my couch, curling my feet up next to me.

"The spend is up to you. The information breach is platinum."

Platinum meant the data transfer level of the information I would harvest was the deepest it went. Usually only government entities or royal families requested this type of hacking. This also meant the microchip tracker I designed had to be of the highest quality and untraceable when installed.

"Client?"

"One of the usual suspects."

We both were quiet for a second and then laughed. The two of us liked to refer to my male counterparts in the hacker world as the "usual suspects," the ones who went rogue and offered their services to the underbelly of the world.

"Understood."

"Standard delivery method?"

"Yes."

"Shoot over the details via the secure network. I'll have it to you tonight."

"Transferring." I heard the click of keys. "Now that we've discussed the assignment, what are you wearing tonight?"

I laughed. This was how it always was with my best friend Devani Patel. We always handled the business aspect of our relationship first.

By day, Devani was a socialite and heiress to a large diamond empire, and my rival in society. Behind the scenes, she worked as Van, an agent for Solon, an underground international organization that would use any means necessary, legal or illegal, to take down the scum of the world.

She was also one of the deadliest people I'd ever encountered. She used her petite size to let others underestimate her abilities, something we had in common.

We'd met while I was in my undergraduate program at

Columbia. One of my professors had dropped my name to a
member of her organization as an up-and-coming expert in
the use of technology to authenticate art. Devani contacted
me to date a sculpture she'd discovered during an assignment. One that turned out to be a forgery and carried a
microchip with information on an organized crime ring.

Over the next few years, we'd become friends and
worked together on assignments that needed discreet tech
investigation. She also became the one person who knew the
most about my plan to take down Uncle Ashok.

"Hold up. We have yet to negotiate my fee." I adjusted
my phone to my other ear.

"Your fee. Does this sound acceptable? I'll double your
standard rate for this last-minute job, and I have a name for
you."

Goosebumps prickled my skin. The last thing I expected
from this conversation was anything to do with my plans for
Uncle Ashok.

She continued, "Are those terms agreeable?"

"Yes." My fingers flexed on the phone. "Now tell me,
who do I need to contact and what do they have on my
uncle?"

"He is someone you know very well." The amused lilt to
her voice had a lump forming in my stomach and a vision of
dark, heated eyes appearing in my mind. "Someone you
watch from afar."

"Nikhil King," I whispered without thinking.

"Very good. As to what he has, I don't know. But my
source says it's something that keeps Ashok Shah's balls in a
vise grip. You are going to have to figure out what it is and
the cost to obtain the information. Any clue as to what it
could be?"

"Hell if I know. But it has to be the root of why Uncle

hates the Kings so much."

"Then I suggest you start working. This is the match that will burn down Shah's house of cards."

I swallowed. "What am I supposed to do? Walk back into Nik's life and ask for a favor? Everyone knows favors from Nik come at a price."

"Yes, that's exactly what you do if destroying Shah is worth it at any cost."

I thought of my parents and everything they'd sacrificed to be together and then answered, "It's worth it."

"And if he wants more than a monetary or business favor?"

"Meaning?" I knew what she meant.

Hell, I'd felt the attraction between us growing ever since Jayna and Kiran had gotten together and Nik had stepped back into my world. The man drew me in a way that no other man had ever done before. It was visceral and unexplainable. And I hated when things couldn't be explained.

"I've seen the way you two eye-fuck each other when you think no one is looking."

"You need to up the prescription on your contacts."

"Come off it. When we aren't playing Van and Dan in our espionage games, we do run in the same socialite circles."

Ignoring her comment, I said, "He's someone I knew from the old neighborhood. A childhood crush, nothing more."

"Who grew into a gorgeous, albeit dangerous, man."

"Let me repeat, meaning?" I cocked a hand on my hip as if she could see me, and then dropped it back onto my lap.

"Meaning, his price could be you. And if it is you, are you willing to pay?"

"First of all, I have to arrange a meeting with him, then I

have to broach the subject of what he has on Uncle Ashok before any of this is even a possibility."

"King is invited tonight. If he shows, step one is set in motion. Then you have to arrange a time for a private discussion."

"I really hate you sometimes."

"No, you don't."

"When do the first games start?"

"Ten."

I lifted my wrist and glanced at my watch. It was already six fifteen. "Not leaving me much time, Van."

"Didn't you say you loved a challenge?"

"Asshole," I muttered. "Bye. I have to get to work."

"Wait. Did you hear the news?"

"If it's gossip, I don't want to know. I have work to do."

"Come on. Humor me."

"Fine. What?"

"There's a rumor the Little Rabbit hacked Manjeet Rai."

I almost smirked at that but kept it in. "Why do I care what's happening on the other side of the world, and to a cartel leader, of all things?"

"I'm just curious. You hackers know everything about each other."

"No, we don't. Hell, most people think Dan is a man. Just like no one would ever think the princess of the Indo-America affluent community is a spy going by the name Van."

It was par for the course when it came to anything of notoriety that a man was given credit. Was it really that hard to imagine women were smart, cunning, or devious?

"Point well made. If you ever find out who it is, please pass the info on. I'm dying to know. This person is my idol.

She or he does all the shit we think about, but without the ramifications to our careers."

"We actually do all the shit most people think about without the ramifications."

"Yeah, but we have to work really hard not to get caught."

"I'm pretty sure it's the same all around."

"I can always hope the Little Rabbit will reveal themselves one day."

"Yeah, yeah. I'm sure they will come out in public just for you."

"Don't pop my bubble."

"Sorry. I'm a realist." I shrugged. "So, back to work."

I had to redirect her thoughts or she would never get off this topic.

"Wait, one more thing."

"Yes?"

"About the delivery method for the tracker, can you do a deeper palette this time? It will go better with my dress. Perhaps a deep burgundy?"

"I'll see what I can do." I almost rolled my eyes and hung up.

Standing up from the sofa, I made my way to my hallway coat closet and pushed aside a set of winter jackets. I stepped onto a pressure sensor and a panel opened. Leaning forward, I allowed the retinal scanner to identify me and the hidden door opened, revealing the heart of my operation. Computers of various types lined one side of the room and a large array of screens jigsawed around another. The back half of the room was set up as a lounge of sorts so I could relax when in the middle of a project without having to leave the space.

I could admit there were times I'd locked myself into what I affectionately called my secret dungeon for days.

Only a handful of people knew about it, people who would die for me before revealing my secret.

Too bad they didn't know all of my secrets.

Pushing the last thought back, I moved to a cabinet in the corner of the room.

The cabinet held preprogrammed microchip trackers ready for jobs like Devani's that would only need a few tweaks for her specifications. With the exception of Devani, most people thought I worked on their projects real time and it kept the demand for my work high because it was assumed they were getting a custom job. In reality, most jobs were standard.

Plus, it would look pretty lame for it to get out that instead of partying it up as most twenty-nine-year-olds would do in their free time, I locked myself in at home and programmed while watching reality television or the latest binge-worthy series on the popular streaming platforms.

No, that was a lie. Well, sort of.

I went out on occasion. But it was rarely, and mainly to serve a double purpose, to be seen in public and to pass off items to contacts as I would do tonight.

After picking out the correct-sized tracker, I exited and locked up the lab and headed for my bedroom. With a quick power-up of my laptop, I attached all necessary cables and devices, reviewed all Devani's notes on my secure network, and went to work. I shook my head, thinking about how I was going to help my girl hack her family's diamond conglomerate. Whatever it was, it was a fair trade as far as I was concerned. I had my reasons for what I did and she had hers.

An hour later, I was set. Leaning down, I pulled open the bottom drawer of my bedside table and hit a hidden button revealing a selection of lipstick tubes. The colors ranged from bright pinks to deep red and everything in between. There were even some wild colors ranging in the blue, yellow, and green spectrum.

Concealing my microchips in the bottom of lipstick tubes kept anyone from suspecting it was more than makeup, and unless you knew the exact way to open the canister, its secret would never reach the light of day. Plus, it helped that the majority of the clients I selected were female.

It wasn't that I was opposed to working for men, I just seemed to prefer working with other women—they understood what it was like to work in a field dominated by men.

Once the unit was assembled, I slipped it into the clutch I'd use for tonight and headed for the bathroom, turning on the shower. As the room filled with steam, I stripped and loosened my hair from the messy but sophisticated bun I favored when at work. As my hair tumbled down my back, I glanced at my reflection in the mirror behind me and smiled. Along my shoulder and down the left side of my body was a unique design of a tigress lying on a bed of exotic flowers. The details of her body were a waterfall of computer code translating a poem my mother would recite to me about the tale of a warrior goddess.

When I'd gotten this ink, I needed something to tell me I wasn't the creature I presented to the world, the creature Ashok Shah had created. It was my hidden rebellion.

And in truth, who would believe the always perfect Danika Dayal's body would bear the marks of a body tattoo?

My attention shifted to the one going down the column of my spine. It held the key to too many secrets.

It was in Sanskrit in its original form, an ancient language very few people spoke and even fewer read.

"Beware of the Little Rabbit."

I'd had it done in New Orleans, when Uncle Ashok had sent me to meet with a potential investor.

It was also the first time I'd gone outside of the realm of hacker for hire. I'd learned a known sex trafficker was in town and decided to help the FBI by anonymously giving one of my contacts the exact locations and codes to the warehouse where the trafficker would be.

It was my way of getting back at those who hurt the innocent.

Among them was Ashok Enmesh Shah.

I guessed everything in my life went back to him. He'd taken so much from me.

My mother.

My father.

Nik.

I knew his connection to people with underworld ties had allowed him to create the empire he currently had. One built on the backs of too many people to count. An empire I'd take from him and give to its rightful heir.

But that was the end game.

First, I had to broker a bargain with Nikhil King.

CHAPTER FOUR

DANIKA

At a quarter past ten, I climbed out of my car, buttoned my long coat, and made my way toward the entrance of The Library, a twenty-four-hour coffee shop favored by the locals of my SoHo neighborhood.

My security detail tailed me. Ones I'd told Uncle Ashok were required by art clients but were actually people I'd hired to keep Uncle's men away from me.

Ever since I could remember, the man had spied on me. And I knew tonight would be no different, especially after the blowup we'd had right before I'd left my apartment.

As if sensing I had plans for the evening, he'd called, demanding I drive over to his house for an important discussion. When I told him I had a meeting scheduled with an art dealer, he'd jumped into a tirade about my lack of duty to the family and how without him I'd have ended up a penniless nothing like my father.

It had taken all of my strength to bite my tongue and listen.

His words weren't anything worse than other things he'd

said to me. At least, they hadn't come with a backhand to the jaw as many of his lectures had ended when I was a teen.

"You're playing with the big dogs tonight. Keep your head in the game," Richard Kade, my head of security and all-around protector, said, bringing me back to the present.

Rich, as I called him, was retired CIA and one of the few people who knew what I really did for a living. Maybe not everything, and if he did, he pretended ignorance well enough.

"I'm always playing with the big dogs. I know what I'm doing."

"Do you?"

I glanced to my side. "Yes."

"Who's the target?" he asked in a low whisper that only I could hear.

Pursing my lips, I glared at him. He couldn't be serious. I answered to no one. Yes, Rich was the closest thing I had to a father, but I wasn't about to give him the details of anything I was doing.

"Do you think they are going to have good cocktails tonight?"

He frowned. "Make sure I have a visual on you at all times."

"I hear you."

I stepped into the coffee shop and approached the bar.

The barista, who knew me, smiled. "What can I get you?"

"Triple shot espresso and an almond biscotti with a strawberry on the side."

"Here's your number. We'll bring it to your table soon." She handed me a blue card and then pointed to a hallway.

Once I paid for my order, I moved in the direction she pointed. After going down a series of hallways, I came to a dead end. I pressed my card to a picture of a rabbit playing cards and a door opened. On the other side, three men stood, waiting for us to enter.

"Hello, Amir." I offered my hand to the breathtakingly beautiful man who managed the secret club I was about to enter.

He brushed his lips across my skin. "How are you, Ms. Dayal?"

"Good. Mr. Danberry is expecting me at his table."

"Yes, he is. He told me to show you in. As always, you know the drill." Amir gestured to the security personnel who waited to make sure Rich and I were clear of any weapons and electronics before entering the premises.

I smiled inside. If they only knew how easy it was to bypass their precautions if one had the right skills.

One day I'd offer the owners my services to truly rid themselves of electronics and weapons.

I nodded and followed their standard procedure.

Once all the security was cleared, Rich went to his normal spot in one corner of the room and I went to greet the people who were in attendance that I knew. The vibe in this room was completely different than of the gala my uncle had held. Here everyone had secrets and it was an unsaid rule that we kept them.

It kind of reminded me of the movie *Fight Club* and its mantra, *What happens in Fight Club stays in Fight Club.*

Anyone who broke the rules suffered the consequences, from the members of the club to the owners. The owners being some of the most dangerous beings on the planet. My research hadn't garnered the full list of owners, but I was well aware the Kings had their hands in it somewhere.

A small vibration in my clutch gave me the signal I needed to make my way to the ladies' room. I excused myself from a group of stockbrokers who seemed to always be in attendance whenever I popped in and searched out the restroom.

Pushing open the door, I scanned the area to make sure I was alone and then walked over to a long chaise on one side of the room and took a seat.

Of course, Devani would make me wait. It was her way. And I guessed in her line of work, it made sense to keep everyone around her on their toes.

Just as I was about to open my clutch and pull out my phone, I heard a door open. A door that I was positive shouldn't exist in a bathroom with only one entrance.

Sighing, I turned to look over my shoulder. Through a bathroom stall that was moments ago empty came a gorgeous brunette. Everything about her screamed "money."

She had it, used it, liked it, and earned it.

"You do realize that a grand entrance wasn't necessary for me."

She shrugged. "What's the point of knowing about a secret entrance into an underground club if I don't get a chance to use it?"

"Sam didn't want to come with you?"

Recently and by accident, I'd learned that Devani and Samir "Sam" King were hooking up. The last thing I ever expected was for them to have any sort of entanglement—they came from different worlds—but then again, so had Jayna and Kir, and those two had fallen head over heels in love.

Surprise flashed across her face. "You're trying to make it something it's not."

What Devani didn't know was that I was protective of Sam for reasons only a few people knew about. He was family. The family I was not allowed to acknowledge. Sam was my first cousin. The son of the woman Uncle Ashok pretended to love, pretended to want to marry until Aunt Monica's family and money came along. He'd seduced the young nineteen-year-old and left her pregnant and alone in a community that shunned unwed mothers.

"What is it, then?"

"It's a mutually beneficial agreement."

"Meaning?"

"He's a King, I'm a Patel. It would never work out. We know what we're doing, Danika. No need to play big sister, especially since we're the same age."

"What are you doing, Devani?"

She glared at me. "We're fucking when the itch strikes. Does that answer your question?"

Her flare of temper said it was more than a fuck-buddies relationship, but I couldn't push it. That was for another time and place.

"Yes, loud and clear."

At that moment, an older woman walked into the lounge.

"Do you have the lipstick you wore the last time I saw you?" Devani asked as she watched the lady walk into a stall. "I swear, I looked everywhere for that shade but could never find it."

Opening my clutch, I pulled out the tube and handed it to her. "Here you go. You can keep it. It's one of my favorite colors and I keep plenty in stock at home. Plus, I think it'll go perfectly with your dress."

Devani opened and then applied the lipstick, pursing and pouting her lips in the mirror.

"This color is on point."

"I'm glad I brought it with me. I had a feeling you'd wear that dress tonight."

To that remark, Devani lifted a brow. "We're overdue for a girls' trip."

"Yes, we are."

The last time I'd gone anywhere was a year and a half ago to Rio.

I was meeting a cyber client and had flown to Lima, Peru in the guise of investigating an art piece for Jayna's gallery. Devani had been lying low between assignments in Guyana. The two of us decided Rio de Janeiro was the perfect place to have an impromptu girls' trip.

We were both in desperate need of a break from our respective lives. She from her crazy money-grubbing family and me from my uncle.

Two short flights later, we were ready for an extended weekend of shopping, beach time, and club hopping.

New York society would never have believed that Shah's niece and the Patel diamond heiress were best friends or that they vacationed together. There was a long history of dislike between our families, something neither Devani nor I could ever figure out the origin of.

Devani's attention shifted from her face to mine. "Damn, girl. You are smoking tonight."

"We're both smoking. It's our MO."

I wasn't a woman who didn't know her appeal. I had inherited my mother's and father's attractive beauty. I knew how to play up my looks when I wanted, even if I preferred the non- glam side of life. It was way easier to throw my hair up in a messy bun and call it a day.

Using our assets was another thing that seemed to bond Devani and me. People, men especially, underestimated us. And that's how we ended up winning most poker nights.

There was no cheating necessary. We were smart as hell, but those around us couldn't get past looking at our tits.

"I have to agree," the older woman who had entered the restroom earlier said in a thick Italian accent. "You are both very beautiful women. I hope your gentlemen know how to treat you."

"We're single," Devani responded as she stepped aside to let the lady wash her hands.

"Not for long, I say. Especially you over there." She gestured to me. "That dress is almost indecent. It's exactly something I would have worn in my day."

She winked in my direction before she left the room.

Devani and I were quiet for a few moments before we burst out laughing.

"I want to be her when I grow up." I rose from the chaise and walked over to the vanity area. "Who was she?"

"Isabella Ricci."

"The card shark?" She was a legend in the poker world. A daughter of an Italian aristocrat who ran away with a gambler and became a notorious card player throughout Europe.

"Among other things."

"I definitely want to be her when I grow up."

"Don't we all." Devani leaned against the counter, looking me up and down. "This dress is beyond anything you normally wear. You're here to play. Are you going to pay up? If a certain King asks a high price?"

There was no bullshitting her. She'd see right through me.

I thought for a second. "I'll do what needs to be done."

She smirked at my response. "Girl, you'll do it, no matter what."

I couldn't deny it. When it came to Nik King, I was in trouble. But there was no way I would let him know it.

There was too much at stake. That man was my kryptonite.

Our past was part of a childhood I couldn't forget. And

he was no longer the kid I knew. He was all man. Dangerous for me.

"I should never have told you about our past. He's a childhood dream I can never act on. No matter how tempting."

"Who the fuck are you kidding? The energy between the two of you is intense. I saw it the other night. Hell, I'd have been surprised if the whole ballroom didn't notice. If given the opportunity, you're going to take it."

"It's a complication I can't add into my life."

"It's inevitable."

"For it to be inevitable, Nikhil King would have to show up tonight, and there is no guarantee he is going to show up."

"Girl, I wouldn't have gone to all this trouble if he wasn't going to show up." I studied her for a second. "What aren't you telling me?"

"Dani, we've been friends for a long time. You know as well as I do, there are some lines we can't cross. This is one of them. Just as you have secrets, I have secrets." She looked at the clock on the wall. "You need to get out of here and meet up with Connor. It's time for me to make my normal fashionably late entrance."

"Call," I said, throwing fifty thousand dollars in chips on top of the pile in the center of the poker table.

"Feeling lucky, Dayal?" the portly man with a thick Irish accent to my right said.

"Luck has nothing to do with it, Connor."

Connor Danberry was a seventy-year-old gamer with a razor-sharp mind that could home in on an opponent's weaknesses within a fraction of a second. He was also a retired

Interpol agent and the man Devani had contacted to add my name to the list of invitees tonight.

Though, if I wanted to join a game at The Library, I wouldn't need Devani's help—a simple call or text from me to Connor would have done the job. Connor had lost a large pot to me the last time we played and he was itching to win some of it back. We had a friendly rivalry of sorts.

"Then are you trying to take out weeks' worth of frustration at the table?"

"Possibly." I gave him a noncommittal grin as I set my cards down.

"Fuck." He pushed the pile of chips in my direction. "I'd normally tell you emotions are the fastest way to lose at the card table but you seem to be cleaning up tonight."

"Aren't you the one who taught me to use my emotions as a catalyst to take out my opponents?"

"Was it me or the man who's staring daggers at me?"

I glanced over my shoulder in Rich's direction. He tried to keep his normal stoic expression in place, but I noticed the slight curve at the corner of his lips.

"I'd say it's up in the air."

Rich and Connor were friends of sorts and had partnered on a few joint international assignments over the years. They had also taken on the role of being my protectors. And because they meant well, I let them. Plus, they had history with my parents. One they felt had prevented the early detection of my mother's cancer and later had led to my father's murder.

"If you win this next hand, I say it's my doing. If you lose, then it's his."

"Would it really be considered a fair game since there are only two of us playing?" I glanced around us and studied the players at all the tables. They were all packed and occasionally players would glance in our direction. "You're making it very obvious that you want to be alone with me. They're going to get the wrong impression."

"Does it really look as if I give two shits what anyone thinks?" He pulled out a cigar from an inside pocket of his suit jacket, stuck it in his mouth, and immediately an attendant came to light it. "Besides, our resident princess and three others are joining us."

I knew Devani was the princess. When she said she was going to be fashionably late, she seriously meant late. And where the hell was Nik?

"Who are the other players?"

"You'll have to just wait and find out."

I almost frowned at his response, but instead asked, "Are you being cagey since you lost the last time we played?"

"Girl, I lost this time too. And for the record, I'm being cagey, as you put it, because it's my prerogative. I'm old as shit and it's my God-given right."

"Fine, deal us another hand. The least I can do is take more of your money while we're killing time."

CHAPTER FIVE

NIK

"All clear," my driver and bodyguard Lake said as I entered the alleyway entrance of The Library around midnight.

Tonight, the tables were packed with high rollers of all types, from the Manhattan elite to those who ran the streets of the underworld. One thing most of them had in common was that they or someone they knew owed me or mine a favor. And then there were those who I called "the others," who were allowed admission because they were useful in various aspects of my family business.

The scent of coffee and baked goods wafted through the air, making my stomach growl. I'd have to order something from the twenty-four-hour bookshop, cafe, and bakery that sat above the club and was owned by one of the King holdings.

The floor manager, Amir, nodded, ready to give me the details on everyone I'd have to meet and handle before I sat at my designated table.

"Welcome, sir." Amir handed me a folder with the list of players and the level of money being played on the floor.

"Lake called ahead to let us know your ETA, and the cafe will deliver your preferred meal any second."

We moved in the direction of the office my brothers and I shared when we made an appearance at The Library. We'd chosen to keep a distance from the place, letting rumors continue working the mystery of who owned the establishment. As far as the public knew, The Library was backed and run by a royal Middle Eastern house—which one, no one knew.

Once we were secured in the office and I settled behind the large industrial-style desk in the back corner of the room, I asked, "Anyone we need to keep an eye on?"

"Nothing out of the ordinary."

I studied him. The response seemed odd, especially because of the request sent from one of my regulars that it was important to make an appearance tonight, and the insistence that I be the brother who showed up.

"Give me the list and I'll make the call on what is out of the ordinary." My tone was harsh but my gut told me by the end of the night, many of the traps I'd set in motion over the years were about to spring and I wanted everyone ready.

"Is there something I'm not aware of?"

Amir was loyal and I trusted him. Well. To a limit. The only people I had complete faith in were my brothers.

"Let's say I came across a tip that something unusual was going to happen tonight."

Amir's back straightened and he started texting. "I've called in extra security and a few more eyes to watch the floor. Nothing is going to happen on my watch."

I almost smiled. My respect for the man went up a notch. His reaction was that of someone who took pride in his job. Amir had come from the same shit neighborhood I'd grown up in and understood the cost of betrayal.

The crazy part was that I wouldn't be the one having to delve out the justice for deception. Those loyal to me would take it into their hands. Each of them knowing I protected my people.

I walked the fine edge of a knife between the world of the legitimate man and that of the criminal, but then again it was a blade I'd balanced on my entire life. If I hadn't learned the dance early, I'd have died within months of my parents' deaths. It was either learn the language and rules of the street or become the victim of it.

"Now give me the player list."

Just as Amir opened his mouth, a knock sounded on the concealed wall panel hiding the door and Lake entered carrying a tray with covered dishes. He set them on the poker table that doubled as a dining table, nodded, and left.

As I moved toward the food and settled in to eat, Amir placed the list in eye view. "The Johnson boys are here, a few of the Wall Street regulars, some of our US and international agency contacts."

The latter in particular was the reason I was here tonight. Connor Danberry. The old coot had insisted I make an appearance if I wanted to catch the one prey I'd had my sights on for years. I hadn't a clue who the fuck the retired Interpol spy was talking about, but curiosity had gotten the best of me. And Connor had always had a reason for everything he pushed me to do. More times than I wanted to admit, his interference had kept my ass from a shit ton of trouble.

"Who are the Dynamic Duo?" I asked.

Amir smirked. "Sorry, I should have changed that when I knew you were coming in. That's what we call it when the socialite princesses come in. Enemies by day, besties by night."

I set my utensils down and glared at him. "Names."

He hesitated, as if he was surprised by my irritation. "Devani Patel and—"

"Danika Dayal," I finished for him.

There could have been no one else. It had to be.

The society gossips loved to play up rumors about some argument the two had gotten into when they were teenagers, but I'd always believed it was bullshit. The Danika I'd known faced things head-on and never let them fester.

I'd seen the proof a little over five years ago, at the Napa wedding of an up-and-coming Bollywood starlet to a high-fashion jeweler to the stars. I'd decided to take a walk along the back of the estate for some fresh air when I'd found the two women laughing and so deep in conversation that they hadn't noticed my presence. Most of the discussion hadn't made sense, a mix of fashion and art. Right before they separated, Danika had handed Devani a lipstick saying that she was right, the color matched her lengha better, and to keep it.

They seemed comfortable around each other. So it made no sense why they pretended not to like each other in public. I'd planned to look into it further but just moments later I'd gotten the call that Arin, my adoptive father, had suffered a fatal heart attack and my world had tilted on its axis.

I'd gone from the eldest of the misfits Arin King had collected off the streets to the ruler of the King empire. In less than twenty-four hours I'd lost my father and taken over his throne to prevent any hungry competitor from absorbing his territory. There had been no time to mourn, no time to think, no time to contemplate how a fucking twenty-six-year-old was supposed to hold together an area amassed over decades.

Pushing the memories back, I said, "I want to know more."

"Sir, I thought you'd be the first to know about them. Isn't Ms. Dayal related to your sister-in-law?"

I clenched my jaw and felt a throbbing in my head. "I obviously missed something."

Which pissed me off to no end.

I couldn't wait until I got hold of my brother Rey. He was our hacker. He was the one who had the information on everyone. Hell, he was the one who was supposed to keep an eye on Danika and her whereabouts at all times.

"They work in the business of connecting people."

"So do I. Want to get more specific? I doubt we work in the same realm."

I wasn't in the mood for long pauses.

"As tech people. Hackers and such. They are very tight-lipped about who the hackers are or if one of them or both of them are the hackers. What we do know is that both of them are tech savvy and that they are physically trained."

"How exactly do you mean, physically trained?"

Next time I saw Rey, I was so going to punch him in the goddamned face for not telling me Danika was a regular at The Library. He knew my history with her.

"Do you remember the incident with Gustov Novak?"

I thought back to the disaster that required a complete shutdown of the club. Novak had threatened to expose one of the guests to her conservative family if she wouldn't escort him home. When she resisted, he tried to manhandle her. She'd pulled a knife that she'd hidden on her body and stabbed him in the gut and then sliced him a fraction away from performing a complete castration. Novak had nearly bled out before the paramedics had arrived. And because of the unwritten code of the club, none of the patrons offered aid to Novak. And afterward, he had all but turned himself into a pariah with his behavior.

Now it all made sense. I'd shrugged off the event as the cost of doing business, especially knowing what happened afterward, when the notorious hacker the Little Rabbit had heard of the Novak incident and decided to get involved. And by morning, all of his financial accounts were drained and his business activities were conveniently packaged and sent to Interpol. Within a week, every one of his known associates who hadn't distanced themselves from him had suffered similar fates.

I'd assumed she was only exacting justice for a wrong done to a fellow female, not to avenge something done to her.

Dammit, Danika.

I should have known she wouldn't limit her activities to hacking, something safe and behind a computer. Someplace where I wouldn't have to get involved and could protect her from afar.

When the Little Rabbit had come on the scene, I'd known her identity immediately. It wasn't just the name, something I'd given her. It had been the causes she'd picked, the people she'd gone after. Danika had a need to destroy everyone who hurt the vulnerable. Always had.

This was just fucking great.

I felt the back of my neck prickle with anger. "Why didn't anyone tell me it was Danika?"

"Mr. Samir, sir. He has a strict rule—if one of the Kings handles the situation, then consider it handled."

Another brother to punch in the face. He deserved it more than Rey. Danika was his actual blood, his baby cousin.

"Are they on the floor now?"

"Yes."

I stood and moved in the direction of the one-way glass disguised as a large oversized antique mirror in the gaming room. Amir followed close behind me.

I had a clear view of the VIP section. Devani Patel sat at a table with Connor Danberry and a group of other men and women. There was one empty seat near Connor I could assume was left open for me. Devani was dressed to the nines as usual in some designer gown that probably came straight off the runway. Devani was a dangerous player. Other players never saw the cunning and deadly creature underneath because they were so enthralled by the package. She was one woman I'd always want on my good side.

Shifting my gaze, I tried to get a better look at Danika with no luck. She was blocked by a man speaking to someone at an adjacent table. All I could see was a heavily jeweled wrist, a bracelet I was very familiar with, comprised of diamonds and sapphires so dark they almost looked black. Immediately, I had the feeling I was about to get a surprise when she finally came into view.

And that was a complete understatement as the man shifted.

God, she was fucking gorgeous. Her lips were painted a deep rich burgundy, her eyes were smoky, and her hair cascaded in long, wild curls down her back. The dress she wore screamed confidence and clung to the incredible body I'd spent more nights fantasizing about than I wanted to admit.

This wasn't the pampered princess from the other night, but a seductress in her element and in the middle of holding court with a group of underworld bosses with ties to international syndicates.

Amir cocked his head to the side as he studied the group. "Do you think she has something concealed on her tonight?

Though she is covered in that long-sleeve gown, it is pretty form-fitting to hide anything."

For a split second, I had the urge to knock his head against the wall for staring at her body in that way. Then I got myself together.

It was his job.

Weapons were forbidden on the premises and everyone went through metal detectors before they went into the club. The fact Danika was able to get anything through my security even once said she had skill beyond the average player. Amir's question was valid.

"I'd say she's been carrying something every time she's been here. And I'd bet Devani is as well."

I had no doubt Danika's weapon was hanging from the long collection of gold chains she had around her neck that dipped down her very low neckline and hugged her full breasts.

My body stirred, knowing the innocent Danika wasn't so innocent. Maybe she wasn't so untouchable as I'd made her out to be. That meant going after her wouldn't be as forbidden as Kir and everyone liked to tell me it was.

"The ladies are cleaning up."

From the look of it, Danika was the one cleaning up with the bulk of the chips loaded in front of her. A large man I recognized from my younger years stood behind her, watching every move everyone made, as did other security sprinkled around the other players at the table.

Danika threw chips into the center of the table and two players folded, leaving the two friends in the game. Danika said something to Devani that caused everyone to laugh and Devani raised the stakes. The women held each other's gazes, neither giving anything away.

No one spoke a word as they set their cards down, face up. Noise erupted around them.

Devani mouthed, "Bitch."

Danika shrugged.

"That's my cue to join." I glanced behind me. "Clear out of here. Before you go, set up a game and then lock all outside access."

"Done."

I moved toward a different set of doors leading into a group of hallways that opened to the bar area of the gaming room.

"Welcome back, Mr. King," the bartender, James, said when I came into view. "Your usual?"

"Yes." I turned my attention toward the tables and my gaze locked with Danika's.

Shock, then something else filled her deep hazel gaze.

She moved in my direction, with smooth, calm, and calculated steps. That damn dress should have been illegal. The fact it was long sleeved only accentuated how low the neckline dipped. If it wasn't for the strategically placed jewelry, the inner curves of her beautiful breasts would be completely on display.

Damn, this woman had me thinking thoughts I had no right to. She wasn't mine. Besides, I wasn't a possessive man.

Hell, with any other woman the rules were clear.

No attachments. No expectations. *No future.*

But then again, no other woman was Danika Dayal.

"Hello, Nik. I wasn't expecting to see you here." Danika set her clutch on the bar and leaned her elbow next to it as she looked up at me.

Though I towered over her in height, there wasn't an ounce of the uncertainty I'd sensed in her only a few nights earlier. The woman before me wouldn't be intimidated.

Which, of the two, was the real Danika? Or were both an act? I planned to find out the answer.

To hell with what Kiran had said. She'd walked into my world and that meant she was now fair game.

From what I'd learned tonight, she spent a lot of time gliding between polite society and the darker depths of the jungle.

"Are you sure about that? There is an empty seat at the table Connor reserved for me."

"There are always rumors of who will show up. I believe things when I see them. Since you are here, I have a business proposition for you." She shifted, reaching over the counter to take an olive from the martini James set in front of her and revealing a slight glimpse of a gold and black design that could only be a tattoo on her shoulder.

She followed the direction of my eyes and straightened, as if I'd caught onto something she wanted to keep hidden.

I touched her shoulder, now covered by her black gown. "I wouldn't think the Shah princess would cover her body in ink."

"I'm not a Shah." Fire flashed in her gaze as she brushed my fingers away and just as fast, I caught her wrist.

"That's right. You're a Dayal, playing in a den full of predators. What are you doing here, Danika?"

"Let me go, Nik." Her pulse jumped under my hold and her eyes dashed to my lips, and instead of wanting answers, I had visions of dragging her to my office and pushing her up against a wall to get my fill of that luscious mouth.

"Are you predator or prey, Little Rabbit?"

She flinched as if referring to her by the long-lost nickname I'd given her had triggered something.

A scared little rabbit had been the perfect description for the eight-year-old girl I'd met on the streets of our shit neighborhood. She'd jumped if anyone spoke too loudly and cried at the drop of a hat.

Why she'd followed me, of all people, around had never made sense to me. I was the mean asshole kid who'd constantly told her to get lost and given her the name Little Rabbit to make her cry more.

But instead, she walked around as if it were the name of a tigress.

"I'm no one's prey, even if I let others believe I am." She freed herself, picking up her drink and taking a long sip before setting it down.

"I'd have to say that was true. You wouldn't have made it past the first night here otherwise, and from what I've learned, you come here often."

"When are you available to discuss business?" she asked, as if I hadn't responded to her earlier statement.

If that was how she wanted to play it. I'd have no problems playing her game.

Picking up my tumbler, I took a slow, healthy swallow and then asked, "What type of business?"

"The kind that will make sure your assets are protected and a mutual enemy is destroyed."

Shah.

"And I assume you are aware my favors come at a price of my choosing?"

"Yes. What I'm offering is more than ample payment."

"It doesn't work that way. I'm the most dangerous of the Kings." I stepped closer to her. "I will take what you offer and then ask for more. The question is are you willing to ante up the cost to achieve your goal?"

She held her ground and my gaze. "Sex between us isn't going to be a business transaction. So, don't try to scare me with those tactics. It won't work. If and when it happens, we'll go in knowing the score."

There she was, the huntress. The woman who seemed to have me in a semi state of arousal whenever I was around her, from the time I was a teenager.

"Oh, it's going to happen. We've circled each other too long. And now that I know you've crossed over the threshold into my world and aren't off-limits, it will happen sooner rather than later."

"Back to the subject, business. When can we meet?"

The fact she hadn't denied us sleeping together was a boldness I hadn't expected.

This woman was one surprise after another.

And my cock approved. Although I could have done without its hard presence in my pants at the moment.

"Wednesday." I reached into my pocket and pulled out a business card, handing it to her. "Be at my office at ten. We'll discuss business then."

CHAPTER SIX

DANIKA

I stared at the card Nik handed me. It was embossed with his name and an address.

Looking up, I stared into his dark chocolate eyes and asked, "What's the catch?"

"There is no catch."

I wasn't buying it. There had to be a catch. But knowing what I knew about Nik, he'd make me wait to find out.

That left the other part of the conversation we'd had that I'd tried to ignore.

Deep breaths, Danika. Fake it 'til you make it.

"And tonight? Do we go to Connor's table and see who's the better player?"

"Cards are definitely on the table but I was thinking to change up the venue." The intensity of his gaze had me wanting to press my thighs together.

God, I was in trouble. Something about him drew me like a moth to a flame.

"Meaning?"

"Meaning a private game, between you and me." The change in his voice had my blood humming.

He was trying to seduce me. Out here. In front of the whole club.

I wasn't that easy, even if my pussy was trying to make a liar of me.

I narrowed my gaze. "Nik, what game are you playing?"

"Besides cards?" He lifted a brow in the arrogant way that should have annoyed me, but instead had my pussy contracting.

Fuck.

"Yes," I said, trying not to give away how my body reacted to him.

"Little Rabbit, the question is, what game are you playing?"

Fifteen years since he'd called me by that name, and in a matter of minutes he'd used it twice. Why was he using that name now, when he'd never done it before in all the years since I left the neighborhood?

He had no idea the power the name had. And the secrets it held.

I shouldn't have picked it as my alias, but then again, this was a private name between two people who destiny had decided weren't meant to be together.

Nik had used it to make fun of the scrawny, frightened girl I'd been. However, I'd also known he'd carried around a small wooden carved tiger his deceased mother had given him named Rabbit. He'd been as much a lost soul as I was and that was probably what made me follow him around and stick with him no matter how much he tried to get rid of the eight-year- old me.

The kids Nik ran with were the ones parents warned their children away from, but they'd become my family, protecting me from the bullies of our neighborhood. And in turn, as I grew up, I protected the boys, especially after Nik took over the crew. I was the studious girl with her nose in a book—the cops would believe me when I said the boys were in a different location than they actually were.

Then everything changed and I lost my world.

Pushing back the memories of the boy I knew, I focused on the man before me. "I have no idea what you mean, Nik."

He set his tumbler on the rim of the bar and leaned forward, his large body all but blocking out the light around me.

"Why are you here, Danika? Why are you friends with men who have reputations for slitting throats as well as fleecing cards? And why did it seem as if you and Devani Patel were best friends when the public believes you can't stand each other?"

Straight to the point, I see.

"My secrets are exactly that—mine. I'm here to play cards. You want a private game. Then let's play."

"Yes, let's play." He offered me his hand.

My immediate reflex was to take it, but a small sliver of sense crept in. If I took his hand, I knew what I was doing. This night was going to end much differently than I'd anticipated when I'd come home from the gallery planning to watch a K-drama.

Hell, it would end in a way that hadn't even been on my radar.

Tonight was supposed to be about getting a meeting; now I was deciding on a game of poker that would end in Nik's bed.

I looked into Nik's beautiful, hypnotizing eyes. He gave nothing away.

Before I knew what I was doing, I slid my palm over his. "Lead the way."

He stared at me for a brief second before lifting my hand to his lips and kissing my knuckles.

Electricity shot through my system and it took all of my strength not to shiver.

"Follow me."

Holding my hand, he moved toward a back hallway. Just as we slid into the dark, I glanced over my shoulder and saw Connor, Rich, and Devani watching us. Each of them with a different expression on their faces. I knew I'd have messages relaying their opinions on my decision, but at this point, I was all in.

The light grew dimmer as we walked farther down the corridor. Just as it grew pitch black, we stopped and Nik placed his hand on a wall plate and a door opened.

We entered an office that I could only describe as a converted speakeasy, with old-fashioned wood paneling, a bar in the corner, and gaming tables at various spots in the room. The only giveaway that it was an office was the large desk sitting in front of a panel of monitors.

"Impressive."

"Rey thinks it is."

"How long have you been connected to The Library?"

"From its inception. My brothers and I own it." He watched me as he gave his answer.

Well, damn. The Kings weren't just tied to the owners, they *were* the fucking owners. It was going to take me a while to get over the fact I hadn't known Nik was behind The Library. I was supposed to be the best when it came to information. I guessed I wasn't the perfect super sleuth I thought I was.

"If Rey wants to upgrade your tech, tell him to give me a call. I'll work with him to make sure you have the best cyber-security available."

Nik stopped midstep, turning slightly in my direction, and narrowed his gaze. "If you ever do business with any of the brothers, it will be with me."

Well, okay then.

Normally I'd have made some smartass remark about possessive men being a turnoff but with Nik, it was a completely different story.

And the fact the close proximity of his body was playing havoc with my head wasn't helping.

"Marking your territory, King?"

He leaned forward as if to kiss me. "I did that over fifteen years ago, Dayal."

Before I could respond, he shifted, moving in the direction of a stocked bar, and poured two drinks. One was a healthy serving of Firewater, a whiskey that cost over a thousand dollars an ounce, and the other was the same amount of Macallan 25.

He brought the two tumblers over to a card table that was ready for a game.

"Here you go. I know you prefer the finer things." He set the Firewater down and gestured to the fabric-covered chair.

I moved to the table and took a seat, letting the slit of my dress ride up so Nik had a prime view of my leg.

Heat flared in the depths of his brown eyes, making my pulse jump. "You do like to play with fire, don't you?"

"I have no idea what you mean," I said as I circled the rim of my glass with the tip of my index finger.

The moment I'd slid my palm across his in the bar, I'd known there would be no going back. We'd circled each other for too long.

Hell, I'd anticipated it, expected it.

But now that I was here, the bravado I'd felt had vanished.

No other man I'd ever encountered had this effect on me. No other man pushed at my control. If I wasn't careful, he'd make me vulnerable, but I needed him for my plan and I couldn't be indebted to him more than I could handle.

"So, the Little Rabbit hasn't learned the dangers of challenging the most vicious predator in the room."

"Stop calling me that. And for the record, don't ever underestimate the rabbit, Nik."

"In my world, rabbits are prey."

I lifted my chin. "I'm no one's prey."

He leaned down, tracing a finger from the hollow of my throat where my necklaces sat to my lips. "I believe you're correct. Underneath the trappings of the perfect society princess is a predator ready to take out everyone who's dared to harm her."

I gave him no reaction. Just stared into his hypnotizing black eyes.

How could he read me this way? It was as if he'd seen into my soul.

This was what made him so dangerous.

Not the fact he dealt in favors. Or the fact he expected something from me and I had no idea what it was. Maybe it was this thing we'd had since we were children. He'd been able to see past my shields to the things I desired most. To the things I wanted to keep from everyone.

I couldn't respond to him without revealing too much. Instead I shifted, removing his touch. One I missed the second it was gone. "Are we going to play or should I go home?"

He rose and then took the seat next to me, his knee brushing my leg. "Is that what you want? To go home?"

There was no going home. He knew it as much as I did.

"I want to play."

"And if your uncle finds out—" he paused and then said with a smirk, "—that you played with me?"

"The only way he'd find out is if you told him."

He lifted a brow with slight amusement. "Don't you think any of the people who watched you leave with me will say anything?"

I shook my head. "Just as I have secrets, they have secrets they want kept hidden. Plus, aren't the house rules, who you see and what you see happen on game night stay within the walls of The Library?"

He set a hand on my bare thigh. "Then you also know the club rule that all debts are paid at the end of the night. No exceptions."

My core clenched and flooded with arousal.

"I haven't lost. It may be you who'll have to pay up."

"From what I learned earlier tonight, you've beaten the house every time you've played."

I could no longer hide the unsteadiness of my breath. His fingers flexed on my skin, shooting sparks up my body.

"We will see if your luck holds out."

Pushing his hand off, I sat back and tucked my legs under the table. "Deal."

"Just so you know. We're playing for clothes."

I glanced to my side. "Strip poker?"

"No. I was thinking something a little different." He shuffled a deck of cards and split it in two, setting a half stack in front of each of us.

I lifted my gaze to his. "Are you serious? Strip war?"

"Why not? It's not as if we haven't played this game before."

The last time was on the steps of Rich's corner shop a week before everything had changed. My young fourteen-year-old heart had felt so much for the boy Nik had been and I'd known he'd cared for me too.

I shook the thoughts back. That was a world away from the one we lived in now.

"Yes, but we were teenagers playing for the deck."

"Very true. This is the adult version where we play for clothes. We aren't going for speed. We flip at the same time, and the high card keeps their clothes and the lower card discards an item."

"I see." I closed my eyes for a second, trying to calm my nerves. I could keep my cool with every other man, but put me in a room with Nikhil King and I lost my wits.

It wasn't as if I hadn't known that things would be anything but simple with Nik—simple wasn't his way. Why would sex be the exception?

We were going to fuck. There was no doubt about that. And when it happened, I had a feeling I was going to relive it for the rest of my life.

The fact he was actually going to make the experience into a game was something I hadn't expected. I'd come in here ready to go along with the farce of playing poker but this was something else.

"Scared, Danika?"

My stomach jumped, feeling his warm breath along my neck.

When had he moved?

Gathering my wits, I glanced over my shoulder and said in the most nonchalant way I could, "Not a chance, King. You're the one who's going to be naked when this is over."

"But you'll be the one begging."

Goosebumps prickled my skin.

Danika, what are you doing? You're playing with a completely dangerous animal. This isn't the Nik you knew.

Ignoring my inner voice of reason, I continued the banter. "Keep dreaming."

"Then, let's play."

Rising to my feet so we were at the same level, we reached for our cards at the same time and turned them over.

My queen of spades beat his seven of diamonds.

Without a word, he reached to his side, settling a small bowl near us, then unhooked his wristwatch and placed it inside.

We flipped again.

His ten of hearts beat my six of clubs.

As I reached for an earring, he shook his head. "I didn't say you could take off jewelry."

"You set the precedent when you took off your watch." I unhooked one double diamond-and-sapphire teardrop piece of jewelry and placed it into the bowl.

"Something tells me that necklace of yours is individual strands." He picked up his tumbler and sipped.

I reached for my cocktail. "You are correct. Twenty strands, to be precise."

"And is there a blade attached to the heavy one in the center?"

He had to have heard about Novak, the rat bastard. No matter what Sam believed, he wouldn't have been able to keep it from his brothers for long, especially Nik.

"I guess you'll have to keep playing to find out." I set my hand on my stack.

We played for the next ten minutes. Somehow, I lost more than I expected and my necklace stores dwindled.

"I don't think you can play this game the same way with that bracelet. It's one piece."

I glanced down at the gift that meant so much to me. Jayna and Kir had given it to me after I'd earned my doctorate in cyber forensics. A degree only they knew I'd achieved.

When Kir had died, I'd lost a brother. Maybe not to the level Nik had, but he knew things about me that I was positive he'd never reveal to any of the Kings. It was a loyalty he shared with me not due to his relationship with Jayna but because he truly cared for me. I owed Kir so much. If it hadn't been for his nagging, I'd never have pursued my graduate degrees.

"How would you know?" I glanced down at the piece on my wrist, twenty jeweled bangles connected by a hidden chain from the inside. It was designed to move as if they were individual pieces but went on and off as one single unit.

"I was there when Kir and Jayna bought it for you."

I swallowed. Kir wouldn't have told Nik why he was buying the bracelet.

"In fact, I told him this was a better twenty-fifth birthday present than the watch they were planning to give you."

"Good choice. I wear it all the time. It also reminds me of Kir." I ran a finger over the diamonds and sapphires.

He set his hand over mine, startling me. "No ghosts in here tonight. Agreed?"

"Yes."

"How about we adjust the rules a bit?"

CHAPTER SEVEN

NIK

I stared into amber eyes that had grown sad as they thought of Kir. I wouldn't let her go down a rabbit hole created by a lie I kept for my brother. One I kept out of loyalty. But a lie nonetheless.

"What rules would you change?"

"How about the winner gets to decide what comes off?"

Her lips curved up in a mischievous grin. "I say within reason. I can veto if it isn't accessible."

"Danika, everything I want is accessible in that dress. In fact, I plan to fuck you with that dress on."

Her pulse jumped under my fingers but she held my gaze.

If I was anyone else, she could have made me believe I had no effect on her. Then again, I knew her. She couldn't hide from me, even if we weren't fifteen years older and hadn't lived a lifetime in different worlds.

"Then I guess we're in agreement."

"Yes, but this time I get the kiss before the end of the game." With one hand still holding her wrist, I threaded the fingers of my other into her hair and tugged her head back before sealing my mouth over hers.

A moan escaped her soft lips as she gripped my neck and deepened the kiss.

God, she tasted incredible, of the unique blend of elder-flower and alcohol from the Firewater mixed with her own intoxicating essence. I'd dreamed of this for years, knowing what it would feel like to have Danika Dayal in my arms. For so long, it had been the fantasy of the seventeen-year-old I'd been that I carried with me but never truly believed would come to fruition.

The press of her tongue against mine had me wanting to push her back onto the table and forget about my plans to draw out the seduction I'd planned the instant she walked toward me in the gaming hall. Instead, I broke our embrace and resisted the pull of her swollen lips and desire- clouded amber gaze.

She stared up at me for a moment before saying, "If I'd known you kissed like this, I'd have kissed you before I asked for that book when I was fourteen."

"I believe it's a skill we've both developed over the years." I rubbed my thumb over her lower lip. "Though I won't deny it would have given me great pleasure to have been your first kiss back then."

"Speaking of books. I never got my book."

"You mean the worthless programing manual that belonged to the library that I stole?"

"Yes. Whatever happened to it?"

I shrugged. "Probably somewhere in the stack of books Rey keeps around in his office."

What would she think if I told her that I knew exactly where that book was? It had been my last connection to her, to the life we had shared before we'd become strangers. I'd hidden it away long ago. Some things were better kept private.

I lived in a world where vulnerability was a weapon and if anyone realized this woman was mine, had always been, life would go from complicated to chaos.

Who was I kidding? Sooner or later, it was going to become public knowledge. Shah had always known it, and for some reason he hadn't leveraged it.

Well, maybe he had.

I studied Danika. She'd always walked a fine line when it came to me. Tonight seemed to be the exception, and I was going to take full advantage.

"I want my book."

Danika's words snapped me back to the present. "Then I guess you need to finish this game and see if our business deal lasts for a very long time."

"I'm not sleeping with you again, Nik. This is a one-night-only thing." She tried to free the wrist I continued to hold, to no avail.

"Keep telling yourself that, Danika." I lifted her hand and set it over her stack of cards. "Let's play."

She opened her mouth as if to say something. Instead, she licked her lips savoring the remnants of our kiss and then said, "Yes, let's play."

I released her hand and went to my pile of cards.

We flipped.

"I win." She tapped the card to her mouth, scanning my body. "Take off your shoes."

I lifted a brow. "Of all the things, you picked my shoes?"

She leaned forward until we were nose to nose. "To eventually see you naked, the shoes have to come off first. Aren't those the rules?"

Fuck. Who was seducing who?

"You're absolutely correct."

I removed my custom-made Italian loafers and reached for my cards.

This time, I won.

She stood, as if expecting me to tell her to take off her underwear.

"Unhook the thick chain and hand me the knife you have hanging from it."

She moved in my direction. "That's complicated."

Setting my hands on her waist, I drew her toward me. "How is that?"

"The necklace is connected to the other two chains and…"

"And," I probed.

"I have to remove the blade before I can unfasten the chains."

Releasing her, I stepped back.

From a slit beneath the embroidery around the lower curve of her breast, Danika pulled a thin, silver dagger with a gold handle. She set it on the table then reached inside her dress. After a click, the gold chains snapped free and she pulled them from around her neck with the blade sheath attached. Gathering the jewelry, she added them to the collection on the tray.

"That's impressive."

"Wait until you get a look at the blade." She picked up the knife and offered it to me with the handle side in my direction.

It was a work of art. The design was a cross between something I would have seen come out of Japan and Germany. It was lightweight, and almost paper thin. The only way this material could have passed through any metal detector was if it had a low metal content, and very few materials existed to have the strength to mold into a usable blade. She had to have paid a pretty penny to have this crafted. Plus, the person who created this piece had to be somewhere between a scientist and an experienced master steel man.

"What type of metal is the blade made of?"

"I'm not allowed to reveal this information. And I never break a promise."

"You are nothing like the woman you portray to the world. I've always known this about you." Something flickered in her eyes, and instead of commenting on it, I handed the knife back to her. "I'd like the craftsman's name. He's remarkable."

"Yes, she is." She slid the blade back into its holder and set the case on the tray. "I'll speak with her and see if she is interested in an introduction."

The way she tossed that out had me wanting to laugh as much as it turned me on. She had so many secrets, and I planned to find out all of them.

She wanted to draw a line, saying this was a one-night thing, but the reality was that neither of us would be able to go back to the way it was. I'd planned to make her mine one day. Danika walking into my world had just accelerated the schedule.

She was strong, there was no doubt about it, but the flash of vulnerability I'd glimpsed grated against my protective instincts.

"Ready to draw?" Danika tapped her deck.

"Ready to get naked?"

"Eventually," she hummed and then flipped her card at the same time as I did. "Take off your shirt."

The way her eyes heated and her breaths grew shallow

made losing well worth it. Hopefully my luck would change and I could work this game in my favor.

But the luck gods were saying, "No dice."

A wicked smile touched Danika's luscious mouth. "It's time for the pants to go."

I stood, giving enough distance for Danika to get a full view, but held her gaze. "You gave the order as if you are a seasoned seductress, but the blush on your face says you are an innocent."

I opened my pants, taking care with the hard press of my cock that was ready to spring free of my boxers.

She licked her lips and swallowed as if her throat was dry, and I had no doubt she was trying to resist looking away from my eyes.

"Nothing to say?"

"I...I'm not sure what to say, other than get on with it." Her irises darkened to a deep golden.

If this is how you want to play it, Danika, I'm master of this game.

Shifting closer to her and taking her hands, I set them on my hips. "Why don't you do the honors?"

CHAPTER EIGHT

DANIKA

My breath caught. He couldn't be serious. I'd barely had my brain functioning after he'd taken off his shirt. His body was a work of art, muscles and tattoos that I longed to touch, and now he wanted me to undress him.

"Go on, Danika. Weren't you the one in the rush to—" he paused, "—get on with it?"

The crisp masculine scent of him tickled my senses, and to finish the task, I'd have to move closer, almost pressing my body to his.

God, he was a large man compared to me.

Boldness and confidence were an art form I'd perfected over the years. But I'd never had them with Nik. I'd bluffed my way through this night with the most dangerous of the King brothers, the only King brother who'd ever made me want more than a friendship, and now it seemed he'd called my bluff.

Moving toward him, letting the skin of my arms press along his, I tilted my head up as he stared down and I pushed his pants down.

Before I could take a step back, Nik took hold of me and caged me against the table, the press of his boxer-covered cock hard against my belly. "Draw your next card."

The thick, aroused rasp of his voice went straight to my pussy.

I drew, not paying attention to anything but the man making my body ache.

"I win."

"Okay," I said without thinking.

"I'm taking off your underwear."

"Okay."

"With my mouth."

"Okay."

When had my vocabulary evaporated to one word?

I gripped his shoulders as he lifted me onto the table, bunched my dress around my thighs, and pressed his thick erection between my spread legs.

He fisted my hair, kissing me as if I were his last meal. It was all-consuming. I felt the power of him all the way to my toes. I was barely aware of my shoes falling to the floor as I wrapped my ankles around his firm ass.

A split second of sanity shot into my mind and I murmured, "This has nothing to do with business. I want to make sure what happens on Wednesday has nothing to do with this."

He pulled back. His eyes gone black.

"This is about us. What was meant to be. You were mine from the moment we met. And now you know it too."

"What?" I tried to comprehend what he was saying but he bit the juncture between my shoulder and my neck, causing me to arch up against him.

"Hill," I gasped.

"Say that again."

Rubbing my cheek against him, I whispered, "Say what again?"

"My name."

"Nik."

He growled and then cupped my breasts through my dress as I drew him closer to my clit with my heels. "No, say Hill."

Had I really said that? The last time I'd called him that I'd been a fourteen-year-old girl, promising my first kiss as payment for a stolen book, a kiss I would have given freely, if only he'd asked.

God, what was I doing?

Nik grasped my jaw, drawing my attention back to him. "You're not retreating now, Danika."

"I'm not."

"I won that round, fair and square." He nipped my lower lip, causing a slight sting before sucking it into his mouth. "Besides, I've dreamt of tasting you for far too many years to count."

"Our game isn't over." I scored my nails over his shoulders in retaliation for the bite.

"We'll finish the game at another time. After I strip you of your underwear, it's time to fuck." He pushed me back until I was lying on the card table. "Any objections?"

He cupped my jaw and leaned over me, and even though I was mostly covered and he was only in his boxers, there was no doubt this man was all power and control.

My pulse hammered in my chest and desire flooded my thong. "Would this end, if I objected?"

"Absolutely. There's always a choice. You will always know exactly what you are getting into with me."

I stared into his dark eyes, feeling the pressure of his

hand on my throat but no fear. "And what am I getting into with you, Nik?"

"You're getting into bed with the most dangerous of the King brothers, Danika." He rubbed his jaw along mine, sending a shiver down my spine. "Once won't ever be enough. You'll crave it, need it, dream about it. No other will ever satisfy your body again."

"Is that a threat?" I tried to sound flippant but it came out anything but as I shuddered and arched into his touch.

"It's a promise." He released my throat and moved lower, nuzzling down my cleavage as he palmed my breasts and pinched the nipples through the material of my dress. "Besides, you'll never want another man to touch you again. And if they do anyway…"

He moved lower.

My fingers slipped into his soft hair. "What would you do, Nik?"

He looked up my body, his lips lifted at the corners. "I'd clean up the mess after you gutted them first."

"You'd protect me?"

"Yes, Danika. That's what it means to belong to me." His words felt like a sucker punch to the gut.

I couldn't trust anyone to that level, especially a man.

"I belong to no one."

He gripped my thighs and tugged me forward. "Keep telling yourself that."

I opened my mouth to respond, but my words caught in my throat when I felt his tongue graze the outside of my knee and trail upward.

Goosebumps prickled my skin, and I curled my fingers into fists. Why wouldn't he let this be some fast fuck instead of a long, drawn-out seduction?

I knew the answer, even if I hated it. It wasn't his style. He was unpredictable; it wasn't his way.

"Now, what do we have here? I know this signature." He ran a finger over the thin line of script hidden in the ink of the tattoo on my thigh. "I want you to lie back, close your eyes, and no matter what I do, don't move."

"Why?"

"Because I want to explore."

"Within reason," I countered. I wasn't sure how long I could wait.

"Agreed. Within reason." His palms slid from my calves, over my knees, until they settled at my hips. The slit of my gown aided Nik's exploration, revealing the drawn-out tail of the animal, mixed into a pattern of mandalas and flowers climbing up my thigh.

"Is this a tail of a tiger, Danika? Can I assume this connects to the ink you tried to hide on your shoulder?"

When I gave a noncommittal "possibly," he began to trace the design, first with his fingers and then with his tongue. I felt everything clench inside.

I shifted to move, but he placed a hand on my abdomen. "Oh no you don't. I haven't removed your underwear."

"N…Nik," I moaned and clenched his hair as his teeth grasped the thin elastic of my thong.

He slowly drew down the fabric, making sure to rub his stubble-covered jaw along my sensitive skin. By the time he had the material down to my knees, I was a panting mess.

"What are you doing to me?" My body ached for more, more than it had with any other man.

I had to remember this was Nikhil King and not Nik the boy I'd known with the completely different last name. This person was all man, one who'd lived a life I knew about from a distance. One that knew how to touch a woman's body.

One with a reputation for giving pleasure. One who'd made it clear he wanted me and planned to make me crave him with every fiber of my being.

No matter what he said, I knew this was my only chance to see firsthand what it would be like to touch his body, to feel him inside me, to lose myself in him.

Tomorrow, I'd go back to the reality of my plan.

One night to indulge.

I could keep it business after this. I had to. There was no other choice, no matter what he believed. I'd worked too hard and for far too long to walk away from my plan for anything else.

"Hill," I cried out when his heated breath blew over my bare pussy, drawing me out of my thoughts and back to the man between my legs.

There was a low rumble in his throat, right before he took a long swipe with his tongue. "You'll be screaming that over and over by the end of the night."

I wanted to fist his hair and arch against his mouth but he grabbed my wrists, holding them in place.

I shook my head. "I want to come with you inside me."

Besides, coming with a man's fingers or mouth took too long, and I was desperate. I needed my release.

"That's a given." His tongue circled my clit. "Fuck, you taste incredible, better than anything I ever imagined."

He shifted my hands to the end of the table, setting them on the edge and giving me the unsaid command to keep them there before taking hold of my ass and lifting me closer to his mouth.

Either from the glorious way his wicked mouth was working my pussy or just from the power of this man, I gave up trying to resist him and let the pleasure fill me.

My nipples strained against my dress as my core quivered with every thrust of his tongue into my soaked channel.

Completely forgetting Nik's command and definitely deliriously lost in the pleasure of his wicked mouth, I grabbed hold of his head, arched up, and cried out, "Yes, right there, Hill. Right there."

The orgasm was fast and hard, and completely unexpected. I writhed against him, rocking and riding the unending peaks of exhilaration.

"Oh God, fuck. How did you do that?"

Nik wiped his mouth against my inner thighs and looked up, lust making his pupils look completely black.

"Don't tell me that a man hasn't made you come with his mouth."

I felt a slight wave of embarrassment. "Not that fast. It usually takes a lot longer."

A smug grin appeared as he rose, threaded his fingers in my hair, and pulled me toward him, covering his lips with mine. The taste of my sweet essence on his tongue was a heady experience.

I reached between us, cupping his straining cock. "Now, Nik. Don't make me wait anymore."

"No more waiting." He thrust into my hold.

Nik reached over my shoulder toward the tray and grabbed a condom. "I'm going to fuck you so hard that you feel me with each step you take tomorrow."

I had no doubt.

He stepped back, pushing his boxers down, a feral blaze in his gaze that had my pussy flooding and clenching at the same time.

I cupped my breasts, needing to ease the ache pulsing all over my skin. This man was beyond anything I could have imagined. I wanted to study him, every sculpted muscle, every tattoo, every scar, but more than anything, I wanted that thick, hard cock jutting out in my direction lodged deep in my core.

"Like what you see?" He gripped his erection, pumping from the root to the tip, precum beading the head.

What I wouldn't give for just a taste of him. There was no doubt he'd be addictive, a forbidden pleasure.

"When you come home with me tonight, I'll let you suck me all you want. Right now I want to bury myself deep in your cunt." He tore open the condom, and just as he began to roll it on, a phone rang.

"Ignore it," I gasped. "Please."

He growled, glancing over his shoulder while fisting his weeping length. "They know better than to disturb me unless it's an emergency."

"Nik, please. I'm fucking desperate." I clasped him with my thighs, urging him closer.

That's when my phone rang, and I stiffened.

"How the fuck does your phone work in here?" Nik's voice went from sex god to ice cold.

I swallowed, inhaled deep, and pushed him back before jumping off the table. "I'll explain later."

I rushed to my clutch. Every fiber of my body continued to rage with need for the man watching me with predatory curiosity.

I wanted to scream at him to answer his own fucking phone instead of staring at me.

While trying to calm my breath, I pulled out my cell and read the bombardment of text messages coming through after the ringing stopped. I followed up with a few coded responses.

The weight of Nik's gaze was heavy on my back as was the incessant ringing of his phone.

Setting my cell down for a second, I grabbed my long hair and fastened it into a loose knot with a band from my purse.

When I couldn't take the ringing of Nik's phone anymore, I shouted, "Nik, answer your damn phone. Shit's about to go down. And I need you to handle things on your end and to stop watching me, for fuck's sake."

He growled something under his breath before barking, "This is King."

The rustling of clothes told me he was dressing in between murmured responses to whoever was on the line, then I felt the press of his fingers as they traced the length of the tattoo climbing up my exposed back.

I should have left my hair down. I'd revealed enough secrets tonight.

"Your man is making it very clear that it is time for you to leave and that I need to shut down for the night. How the fuck does he know this? Want to tell me what's going on?"

Ignoring how amazing his fingers felt, I glanced over my shoulder and said, "Your first- timer, Peterson on table fifteen, lost big tonight and decided to become a police informant. My contact sent me a message."

I showed him some screenshots on my phone of the guy in question and other details. "You'll have all of this information on your computer within the next few minutes."

"I would have heard about this."

"Nik, we don't have time for a detailed discussion on what you should have known." I turned back to my phone, pulling up an app I'd developed with a few friends that wasn't technically legal. "I'm accessing their servers to adjust their information and also to piggyback the locations of all the places called The Library across the city with the same MO. By the time they come here, the only thing they'll find is the cafe and the storage area underneath. Are we clear?"

That came out bossy, but I was saving his ass and there was no way around it. He'd just have to deal with it.

When I turned, suspicion filled his dark eyes as they bore into mine. "Who do you work for, Danika?"

"Everyone and no one."

"Why are you protecting me?"

Without hesitation, I gave him the truth. "Isn't that what I've always done?"

"Protecting me is dangerous." He stepped closer, gripping my waist and drawing me toward him. "And it could bind you to me in a way you may regret."

Pretending he hadn't spoken, I braced my phone and hands on his chest. "You need to clear this place. You have an hour. If that."

A line formed between his brows. This wasn't the time to discuss anything serious other than the fact he was about to be swarmed with cops.

"Wednesday, we discuss business. Then we finish this," he emphasized by biting my lower lip.

I resisted the moan that wanted to come out at the light sting.

Before I could respond, he continued, "And when I say finish, I don't just mean the sex."

"Fine. Wednesday. Now do as I've told you."

He held me, not giving even a sense of urgency at the situation he was in. "Danika. I believe I need to make something very clear to you."

I glared up at him. "What?"

"You're mine. I'm not pretending anymore. Fifteen years we've played this game. No more."

"And let me make this clear. I belong to no man."

At that moment, a pounding started on the door.

"Nik, time to turn over the building," one of Nik's men shouted. "The crew is arriving."

"I'll see my way out." I slipped from his hold and moved to the wall panel we'd entered through.

"Danika. What about your clothes and jewelry?"

"We'll see each other Wednesday. I can pick it up then." Pushing open the wall, I stepped through it to find Rich waiting for me with my coat. A crease formed between his brows as he took in my appearance.

I slid my arms into the coat, followed him to the exit, and slipped into my waiting car.

Neither of us said a word. I'd hear a lecture later, but now wasn't the time.

Besides, I had enough on my mind.

And most of all was the fact that there was no going back to the way things were with Nik, with him at a distance.

I'd revealed too much, too soon.

It was supposed to be sex. Hell, we hadn't even had sex. Not in the conventional sense, and my body was still on fire for him.

Then there were the many questions I'd seen in his eyes. Questions I knew he was going to push for me to answer until he was satisfied.

And would I give him the truth or a version of it?

I was well and truly in over my head.

I should have stayed home, drunk wine, and watched K-dramas.

CHAPTER NINE

NIK

I entered my penthouse at a little past three in the morning. I was bone-tired and ready for a stiff drink. What should have been a night ending in losing myself over and over again in the curvy body of Danika Dayal ended up being a cluster fuck of smoke and mirrors to keep The Library the illusion it was.

And when it came to illusions, that's exactly what Danika had become. The second her car left the street of the club there'd been no trace of her.

My men insisted her car vanished.

Which was bullshit.

They were supposed to be the best. Then again, they'd never gone against former CIA operative, Richard Kade, when he was protecting his ward.

Instead of handing my crew their asses when they returned, I'd let them deal with the turnover of the club, something they'd trained to do within a twenty-minute time frame but never actually had to pull off until tonight.

This also meant I owed one to Danika.

Would she put this in the jar of debt she'd collected from

me when we were kids or add it to a new one? Back then, the beat cops who strolled our neighborhood viewed Danika as the nerdy, quiet girl. If she said something did or didn't happen, it was the truth.

I used to believe the cops were stupid as fuck for listening to Danika every time she said she hadn't seen us, or had put us in a spot we weren't to keep us out of trouble. Later on, I'd realized it was their way of looking the other way to protect us too. Those guys had grown up on our same streets and instead of going the darker routes of our neighborhood, they'd gone the straight and narrow.

Well, mostly.

Moving to my bar, I poured a healthy glass of scotch and downed it before filling it again and walking toward the floor-to-ceiling window overlooking the night sky.

As of now, the fucker Cameron Peterson was blacklisted from every establishment in the gaming world. His beloved family's name or going to the cops wouldn't save him from paying his debts.

The idiot had no clue making an enemy of me had lasting effects.

Cameron's father had sent me multiple messages saying he'd pay back triple his son's debts, if only I continued to help him with his building project.

And there was the crux of what my brothers and I did for the world. We were the middle man between legitimate society and what people would call the unsavory element. People loved to throw around words like unions and contractors and codes; they tended to forget behind all of this were people. Everyday, living-paycheck-to-paycheck, looking-for-their-next-meal people. And because I took care of these men and women, I had their loyalty, giving me the power to make or break any investment made in a territory my brothers and I ran.

I wasn't some fucking Robin Hood. Half the shit I engaged in wasn't technically legal, but then again, neither was the everyday sea of transactions those Wall Street boys wheeled and dealed in. The only difference between us was that I owned what I did, while they pretended they were above reproach.

Just like our boy Cameron. Dumb fuck.

I'd deal with him and his father after a night of sleep.

Setting my tumbler on a nearby table, I reached into my pocket and pulled out the ornately designed sheath and knife. It was so much lighter than I expected. Sliding the blade out of its holster, I studied the craftsmanship and shook my head. I was getting hard thinking of the fact Danika had this nestled down her breasts most of the night.

Who was I kidding? My cock hadn't settled since her fingers had wrapped around me and urged me forward. I'd probably remain this way until I fucked her senseless or punched the shit out of someone in the ring.

Both were inevitable. Though the boxing ring looked to be the closest to coming to fruition.

Wednesday.

I'd wait until Wednesday and then Danika Dayal was going to be mine.

I'd kept my distance to protect her, and what had that gotten me? A woman who wrapped herself in secrets that could get her killed if anyone found out the truth.

Anyone meaning someone like me.

Another motherfucker like me would manipulate her, keep her, and make sure she was indebted so deep that her secrets would never reach the light of day.

For her sake, I pretended to be like everyone else and accepted the package she presented to the world.

Now that I knew how dark and deep her path went, all my noble intentions were gone.

The image of the tattoo down her spine came to mind and I shook my head.

Fuck, Danika. I will not let anything happen to you. That's a promise.

Secrets. So many secrets.

"Did you fuck her?" an irritated voice said from the shadows to my side.

"This *Phantom of the Opera* shit is getting old. You can turn on the lights if you're going to invade my space." I kept my gaze on the blade. "And, no. I didn't sleep with her. Not that it's any of your business."

"Don't lie to me."

"If you are going to watch the monitors like a peeping tom, then you might as well stop hiding in the shadows."

"You're an asshole."

"Yeah, and what? I doubt you could do anything about it. You're too scared of your own shadow to train with the rest of us in public."

Kir shot toward me, slamming my back to the glass wall. "If you want a fight, I'll give it to you."

"Go ahead," I said as I kept still and stared into the rage he so rarely let out. "Try me. I've spent most of this evening doing your job instead of spending it with Danika finding out what shit she's been up to."

He released me and walked back to his chair in the corner. "What the fuck do you mean by that?"

That was typical Kir. One minute he was ready to hand out a beatdown and the next, he was calm as fuck, ready to analyze the situation.

"Which part? Danika or your job?"

"Both."

"Let's start with your job. We need you back, not watching everything from the backend. Your presence keeps people from fucking around."

"It's not the right time."

"It's never going to be the right time." I leaned against the window. "Then there is Danika."

"What about her?"

"I've decided that she's mine. No more waiting."

"I swear Nik, if you hurt her, I'm going to kick your ass."

"Be my guest."

Kir sighed. "If Arin was around, he'd knock some sense into the both of us."

One of the last images of Arin before he died flashed in my mind. He had a stern expression on his face, matching the serious styling of his stark gray hair. The only thing that gave any inkling of his feeling about any of us was his eyes. Hazel with light flecks of gold. They softened whenever my brothers and I entered a room.

"Definitely."

"It's been five years and it feels like yesterday."

"Yeah." I had no idea what else to say.

To Arin, we weren't the street rats who tried to pick his pocket, but the boys who were his sons.

"Where do you think we'd be if we hadn't decided to fleece Arin?"

"Probably dead or in jail." I couldn't deny the truth.

It had been fate that we decided to hustle him the very day Danika disappeared.

Well, maybe not fate but more in response to my anger at Danika for vanishing before I could collect on the kiss.

When I'd gotten to the shop to deliver the damn book,

Old Man Kade, aka Agent Richard Kade, told us Danika was gone and she was never coming back.

Instead of finding out what happened to Danika, I decided it was time to fleece the wallet off the rich dick who walked the neighborhood as if he owned it. Back then, I hadn't realized that Arin actually owned most of the properties in the area.

I'd come up with my idiot plan without thinking through any of the consequences. Kir, Sam, and Rey were supposed to distract Arin by bumping into him as they ran down the street. I'd walk by at the same moment and snatch Arin's wallet.

It would've all worked out perfectly, if I hadn't fucking tripped.

One of Arin's bodyguards grabbed me by the neck and his other protection knocked the boys to the ground. I assumed we were going to die by the end of the night. It would have been better than to walk by the shop and not see Danika there. But as we rode in the dark limo going to a place I'd assumed would be our final resting place, Arin offered us a deal none of us expected.

He gave us the choice to go to jail, to die, or to join him and do everything he told us to do. In return, he would teach us how to work the streets without running stupid games, and we'd never have to worry about a place to live again.

It was an opportunity only an idiot would refuse. And there was one thing very true about all of us—we were poor but not idiots.

"Arin saved us," Kir stated.

"Arin would say we saved ourselves by getting our heads out of our asses and listening to him."

Arin's teaching methods could only be described as unorthodox. He taught us everything he knew. From hustling a man on the streets to negotiating a deal with Wall Street suits.

He played the middle man between the underbelly of society and the so-called legitimate businessmen, dealing in favors, ones he would hold on to until the perfect opportunity presented itself.

I'd taken to the life faster than my brothers. Probably because I'd dealt in the currency of favors even before I learned anything from Arin. I intuitively knew having others indebted to me meant I had power.

I also had no real ties to family. Outside of Aunt Beverly, a distant relative from my mother's side who took me in after my parents' deaths, I had no family. And I wouldn't have described living with Aunt Bev as the ideal situation. She was in her late sixties and overworked with no time for a kid. She provided the bare minimum and let me do as I wanted.

I honestly believe she was relieved when Arin told her he was taking me and asked her to sign over her rights.

If I was honest, I hadn't made it easy for her. I had a knack for finding trouble and a reputation for fighting authority.

"He never minced words." Kir stood, walking over to the bar and pouring a healthy serving of Firewater.

Immediately I had a vision of Danika's rich painted lips wrapped around the rim of her tumbler sipping her whiskey. There was no doubt in my mind that until the day I died, I'd associate the elderflower-infused spirit with the sexy-as-sin siren with too many secrets.

"Want some?"

I shook my head. "You do realize that's over a thousand dollars'-worth of alcohol in that glass."

"It's not as if you can't afford to get more. Besides, if it wasn't for my wife, you wouldn't have it."

I couldn't argue that point. It was Jayna's contract with Penny Lykaios, the inventor and distributor of Firewater, that had gotten me access to the extremely hard-to-acquire liquor.

After swallowing a healthy gulp of the whiskey, he asked, "How would Arin tell you to handle the Dani situation, whatever it is?"

I thought about it for a few seconds, shook my head, and laughed. "He'd say play the cards you're dealt. Meet the challenge with your own and don't back down for anything."

"In other words, you're going to do whatever the fuck you were planning to do in the first place."

"Yep."

"Want to elaborate, asshole?"

"Sure. I'm going to let her come to me with her business proposition and then I'm going to counter with my own."

"Nik. Fucking her isn't going to be part of any bargain you make." There was a warning in his words that would have scared a lesser man and someone who wasn't one of his brothers.

"You're right, fucking her isn't something I'd ever include as part of any bargain with her. It's something that's going to happen no matter what anyone has to say about it."

"Don't take out the past on her. It's not as if she had a choice when she left. Besides, it was a better life."

"Was it?" I countered.

He knew the truth. He knew what happened inside the walls of the Shah mansion. He'd read the reports from the investigators Arin had hired to keep a watch on Shah, if he hadn't gotten a first-hand account of life as a Shah princess from Jayna.

"It was better under his roof than living like we had. All I'm saying is that she's been through enough."

"Give me some credit." I couldn't hide my annoyance. "The last thing I'd do is intentionally hurt her. Hell, I kept my distance for that very reason."

"Then what are you planning?"

"The same thing we originally intended. To protect her. Something we haven't been doing, if she's been running with the likes of us for the past who knows how long."

"What the fuck does that mean?"

I lifted my glass in my brother's direction. "I'm going to marry her and make sure she can never walk away again."

CHAPTER TEN

DANIKA

"A few more clicks and I'm in," I mumbled through a yawn.

This was the best part of my job. Getting to hack companies legally. Well, maybe not so legal in this case, but it was for a good cause.

The fact I was too damn tired to enjoy it sucked. I'd had less than three hours of sleep and was running on fumes.

Some of it was my own fault for staying up to finish this project and only taking cat naps while my program worked through various firewalls but the other...

Well, that was...

I hummed to myself as visions of Nik's golden, tattooed, muscled skin came to mind. Along with his wickedly talented mouth. And let's not forget those hypnotizing eyes that seemed to push past my defenses.

My body hadn't stopped aching for the man I'd dreamed of touching for most of my life.

I still couldn't believe I'd let things go so far and revealed so much.

Could I trust him to keep my secret or would he use it against me?

Fuck!

I guess I'd find out soon enough.

Picking up my mug of lukewarm coffee, I wrinkled my nose before chugging it down. I really needed to invest in one of those mug-warmer things Jayna kept on her desk when analyzing art in the office. There was something soothing about having a warm drink on hand at all times.

After setting my cup down, I grabbed my phone and dialed Devani's number.

"Morning, Dan," Devani said over the sounds of pots. She was probably making her ritual cup of chai, a tea made of milk, water, and a mild blend of Indian spices. "Please tell me you didn't leave Nik King's bed just to work the rest of the night."

"I never got in his bed."

"Don't burst my bubble like that. I assumed you left with him following the chaos of clearing the club."

"Not my style. He handled business and I went home."

"Idiots. The both of you."

"Hey. What the hell does that mean?"

"It means you two have circled each other for years and when you get the chance to bone, you walk away."

"He had other pressing matters."

"I think it was you. I know you. He would have let his men handle things. You're scared he's going to have you cock-whipped."

I rolled my eyes. "Yes, that's it, Dr. Phil. I'm scared that Nik King is going to have me cock-whipped, so I let him dazzle me with his incredible magic tongue and then nearly fuck me before we were disturbed."

Shit, had I just said that?

"Wait, what? You nearly fucked in the club? Oh my God. Danika Dayal, you rebel, you."

"Ignore you heard anything. I'm going to hang up now."

"The hell you are."

"Dammit, Van, I am not discussing my sex life right now."

"You haven't had a sex life in years so let me have some fun."

"No. Now back to the reason for my call. Is everything ready on your end? I'm ready to activate."

"Yes. I had a feeling you were going to finish this project before the ten a.m. deadline. Let me send the team a message." She paused for a few seconds. "Okay go ahead, they're ready when you are."

"Okay, in three, two, one." I hit the last of the codes for my software to go live. "System streaming."

A series of encrypted lines of code filled my screen, a duplicate of what was transmitted to the network on Devani's end.

"As always, the agency appreciates your assistance. Payment for your services is on its way to your account."

By noon today, I'd be five hundred thousand dollars richer. Well, my Swiss bank account would be.

This job was completely different than the one I'd done for Devani yesterday. It involved my services for a quick investigation into a financial firm in Alberta they suspected to be a front for funneling cash to a drug cartel. This was low key, low risk, and easy money. A no-brainer, in my book.

"All in a night's work." I sighed, shutting down my computer and sliding it into the hidden compartment in my couch. "I'm hanging up now so I can get some sleep before I have to head to the gallery for an interview."

"Oh yeah. The new analyst I recommended." There was a tinge of humor to her voice. "Lilly Lennox."

"Yes. She's looking for a fresh start and I think we're the best place for her."

"Does Jayna know about her background?"

"What part? The fact that she is in the same profession as I am, that her father is a German mob boss, or that she just got out of a toxic relationship?"

"Yes."

"Jayna has all but checked out from the gallery. I make the decisions. Besides, Jayna isn't going to object to hiring Lilly."

"I swear the two of you are nothing but bleeding hearts."

"I'd say you're no different, since you're the one who put her on my radar."

"Point well made. Time for me to put on my heiress hat—I have to go to a shareholders meeting. Bye."

"Bye."

I set my phone on the coffee table, stood, and stretched, feeling the snap and crackle of my joints from sitting in one spot for too long.

My phone rang, making me groan.

What now?

I read the display, seeing it was Rich.

I answered with, "I was just about to crash, make them go away."

"I take it you stayed up instead of getting some sleep as I advised?" There was a hint of amusement in his question.

"Something like that," I muttered.

"You have a guest. Do you want to come down or should I send him up?"

I sighed, wanting to say neither. The only reason he

would ask the question was if it was someone I knew. My energy was down to critical levels.

And I knew it couldn't be a potential security client. They could only contact me through specific channels.

Maybe it was for the gallery. It occupied the first floor of the eight-story brownstone warehouse I lived in. A building no one outside of my immediate circle knew I owned.

"Who is it?"

"Your uncle."

I closed my eyes for a brief second. Nothing made a day tank like a visit from dear old Uncle Ashok. Then again, I should have expected something like this, especially since I all but blew him off last night for my visit to The Library.

"I don't suppose you could tell him I was dead or had the plague or something?"

Rich remained silent.

"Fine. You spoil all my fun. Have one of our guys bring him up. And make it clear that none of his men are allowed past the lobby. I don't trust any of those assholes."

"Will do."

"And one last thing. If I shoot him for coming between me and my sleep, I expect you to clean it up and hide the body."

"Of course, it's part of my job description." Rich hung up.

I pinched the bridge of my nose, taking a few deep breaths and getting into character to handle whatever Uncle Ashok wanted.

I glanced at the clock on my living-room wall. I had ten minutes before he made it up to my penthouse.

Thank God I'd listened when Rich insisted I have everyone who wasn't on my safe list screened before access to my personal floor. When I'd bought the warehouse a decade ago for a bargain, I'd done it for Jayna—she'd needed a place for her gallery and seed money to purchase her appraisal equipment. Uncle Ashok had blocked every opportunity she'd gotten to fund her business, including threatening any financial institution with the loss of his business if they dared to give her a loan.

By this time, I had a Swiss account loaded with money I'd earned as a freelancer for Solon and other clients so I decided it was a great way to give a big fuck-you to my uncle.

Plus, working for Jayna and living in the supposed "subpar" apartments above the gallery worked in my favor to keep the image of a poor Shah relation. One of the things I'd learned over the years was that if I acted the dutiful and appreciative niece, he'd leave me alone. Well, for the most part.

I shook my head and went into the kitchen to make up a tray of tea and sweets for our esteemed guest.

The shit I did to keep this fucking image.

The doorbell rang, and I glanced down at my yoga pants and Star Wars shirt.

Oh well, he'd deal with my unrefined look.

Releasing a sigh, I opened the door.

Instead of saying hello, Uncle Ashok walked in as if he owned my place and said, "I think it's ridiculous for me to have the help pat me down and put me through a security scan every time I visit."

I glanced at Talia, one of the guards who worked under Rich. She nodded and motioned she'd wait outside for him.

I closed the door and said, "I don't have a choice, Uncle. The museums and art collectors require it as part of our contracts for insurance purposes."

The security served a double purpose—keeping the high-priced art safe and making sure my uncle couldn't bug the building as a way to keep an eye on me. I'd had no privacy during the many years I lived under his roof and refused to go through that again.

When Rich had suggested these security measures, I'd jumped at the chance. He was ex- CIA and one of the few people I trusted completely.

He knew more about me than nearly anyone. Hell, he'd been part of my life for as long as I could remember. Back in the day, I'd called him Old Man Rich. He'd owned the corner shop where I spent my time in the old neighborhood.

It wasn't until I was an adult that I'd learned that Rich had been Papa's handler—well, until Papa was murdered. Murdered investigating Uncle Ashok and his international business dealings.

I'd assumed after I left the neighborhood, Rich would never be part of my life again. Uncle Ashok had forbidden me from having any contact with anyone from my past. But Rich had never stopped watching over me, even if it had been from a distance.

Then during my freshman year at Columbia, Rich stepped into the cubby I'd reserved for the afternoon at Avery Library. It still made me smile to think of how Rich had just walked in and taken the seat across from me as if he was my study partner.

The library was the one place my uncle's surveillance wouldn't follow me. The men sent to watch me assumed I couldn't get in trouble if I had my head in a book.

That day, Rich had revealed what his real relationship to Papa had been.

Needless to say, I'd been shocked. Papa never gave one clue he was anything more than a mild-mannered currier who hoped to be an engineer, and it was hard to imagine he was working with the CIA. Rich also told me that he'd made a promise to watch over me and planned to continue doing it.

I'd been annoyed with having another person spy on me, but Rich had calmed me down by saying as long as I wasn't in danger, he'd let me live my life and make my own decisions.

"I'll never understand how you can make money looking at splatters of paint all day." Uncle Ashok's voice snapped me out of my thoughts, and I focused on his face. "Or have the means to hire a staff."

"Some of my clients pay well to make sure they are buying authentic artwork."

"You're wasting your scientific mind. You should have gone to work for a tech company. Then your talents would be put to good use."

Instead of responding, I went to the counter, picked up the tray, and brought it to the living room.

Uncle Ashok gestured to the table and I placed it on the wood. He took a seat and waited for me to join him.

He loved to play lord of the manor, and I'd go along for now. At least until he pushed me too far.

"There is something you're going to do for me." He lifted his mug and took a sip of the tea.

I waited for him to continue.

"Nikhil King has information about my business. I want you to get it for me."

I furrowed my brow. He couldn't possibly mean for me to hack Nik. No one in the family knew what I did on the side. Well, Jayna, but she wasn't part of this equation.

"I'm not following. You specifically told me I'm never to have any association with him."

From the second I stepped foot in Uncle Ashok's

mansion as an orphaned fourteen-year- old, I was told to sever ties to the "thugs" I'd spent my time with.

To my regret, I'd done exactly that, not wanting to lose my only living family, and learned quickly I was the substitute for my mother, Reka, who'd run away to marry my father. Uncle Ashok controlled everyone around him, especially his wife and daughter. With me in the mix, he planned to make sure I never made the mistakes his sister had.

"Yes, but King is interested in you, always has been. That means we can use it to our advantage."

"He was my friend when I was a child, nothing more."

"Don't play coy. I saw you looking at him."

"I was keeping an eye on Jayna, not H…Nik."

Fuck, I'd almost called him the name I'd given him a lifetime ago. A name I hadn't spoken in nearly fifteen years until last night. I couldn't slip up again, especially not around Uncle Ashok.

Hill was the boy from my past, Nik was the man.

"Well, he couldn't keep his filthy attention off you."

"I'm not following. How do you expect me to get this information?"

"I want you to seduce him."

I coughed, not expecting that. "You what?"

"I want you to make him fall for you and then get him to send me what he has on me as a favor to you. Since you'd already be sleeping with him, he won't expect more from you."

He had to be out of his mind.

"You want me to whore myself for you?"

I had to be in the Twilight Zone. The last thing I ever expected was this.

When Jayna had fallen for Kiran King, Uncle Ashok had been angrier than I'd ever seen. And then, when he'd learned his little girl had eloped, he'd all but lost his mind, raging about having to take matters into his own hands to eliminate the unsavory element that dared to tarnish his daughter.

Then a year later, Kiran had his accident, leaving Jayna a widow. Something I was sure Uncle Ashok masterminded, even if I couldn't prove it.

"I'm telling you to protect your family. It's the least you can do for taking you from the hovel you lived in before your worthless father got himself killed."

I tried to rein in the fury burning inside me at the mention of Papa. It was easy to mask my true feelings in every situation except when it came to my parents.

"How does whoring me out protect the family? You said Jayna ruined herself by marrying Kiran and now you want me to fuck his brother. Does my reputation have no value?"

"You will do this, Danika." Anger flared in his eyes. "I have something you want and if you ever expect to get it, you will do this."

I closed my eyes, seeing my mother's weak smile as she lay in the hospital bed, her body ravaged by cancer and chemo. I'd been eight. She'd told me she'd written letters that I was supposed to get on my sixteenth birthday as part of my inheritance from her.

I was too young to understand what she meant. It wasn't until after both Mummy and Papa passed that I learned that half of what Uncle Ashok claimed as his fortune had belonged to my mother.

I couldn't have cared less about the money. All I wanted were her letters.

I clenched my teeth and let the anger I held in show. "So, if I fuck Nikhil King to get this information, you'll give me the letters?"

"Yes."

Liar.

"I'm not selling myself on the chance I'll get them. You want to bargain. Let's bargain. I want the chest and the letters, first."

"My word is good enough."

Like hell.

"No, Uncle. You've told me this lie too many times. I won't let you hold them over my head any longer."

I clenched my teeth.

I couldn't do this charade anymore. What was the point anyway? I wasn't an idiot and I was acting like one. I knew I'd never get the letters or the inheritance that belonged to Mummy unless I took it. This was the reason for the plan.

I couldn't use the excuse that I was playing his puppet to protect Jayna. She'd blatantly told me she didn't need my protection anymore.

I'd lost so much because of this pathetic man.

He wanted what Nik had. Well, I wanted it too. And the hell I was going to give it to him.

"You ungrateful girl. How can you say that after all I've done for you?"

"Do you mean like keeping the money Mummy was supposed to get as part of her inheritance that you used instead to further your hotel business?"

"If your mother had followed directions, she wouldn't have needed it."

Ignoring him, I continued. "How about holding those letters over my head to keep me in line." I stood, stalked over to my door, and opened it.

Talia waited there.

"Get out, Uncle. I refuse to let you turn me into a whore only for you to throw something else in my face."

"You dare to talk to me like that? I'll make sure you regret it."

At his words Talia moved toward me, ready to come between my uncle and me.

I shifted, so I faced him fully. "What can you do? I haven't taken a cent from you since I graduated high school. I went to college on scholarship with a living stipend and then went to work for Jayna. If I owe anyone anything it is to her. Your daughter, the child you threw away, is the one who saved my ass."

He rose, coming toward me with such force, I knew he expected me to cower as I'd done so many times before.

Instead, I stood my ground and braced for whatever he thought he could do to me. What the fucker had no clue about was that I wasn't that weak, untrained girl anymore. I'd fuck him up.

He grabbed my face, but before he could say anything, I pulled the gun Talia kept at her waist and pressed it to Uncle Ashok's stomach.

"Let go of me."

He squeezed tighter. "You don't have the guts."

"Try me." I stared him in the eyes.

"And you think no one is going to hear a gunshot."

I smirked. "The gun has a silencer. I'm ten times smarter than you believe. And Talia is former Mossad. She'll help me make it look as if you were mugged in another area of the city with no trace of your visit here."

He glanced at Talia, who shrugged.

"Don't make an enemy of me, girl."

"And tell me, Uncle. When have we ever been friends?"

He stared at me and then abruptly released me. "This isn't over. I've worked too hard to get to this point. I will not let you and definitely not a King stand in my way."

At that moment, Rich appeared, grabbing my uncle. "Mr. Shah, your presence is no longer welcome here."

He said nothing further as Rich led him away.

I watched the empty corridor as the first wave of nausea washed over me.

He'd done it. He'd finally pushed me too far. And I had no doubt I would have pulled the trigger.

Talia set a hand on my shoulder as if to comfort me, and then in a blink of an eye had the gun out of my hand and back in her holster. "Sit. I'll get you some water."

In a daze, I went back to my couch, dropping my face into my hands. "What the hell did I do?"

"You stood up for yourself. It's about damn time, if I do say so myself."

"Did I make a mistake?"

"No. He was going to force you to do something that went against everything family is supposed to ask you to do."

"So, I guess you heard everything that led up to the gun incident?"

Talia handed me a glass. "Only if you wanted me to hear it."

"Smartass." I glared at her and then smiled. "What now?"

"That's up to you."

I thought for a minute and then sighed. I knew what I had to do.

Accelerate my timetable.

And that meant push to meet with Nik sooner.

When I saw him, the events of last night had to remain separate as did our past. I couldn't think of him as the boy who protected me when life had taken so much from me. He wasn't my friend, the one person I could count on, or my first love.

He was a means to an end, a business associate who had as much to gain by ending Ashok Shah as I did.

I grabbed my phone and dialed Jayna's number.

After two rings, a soft voice answered. "What's up, Dani? Got a new project for me?"

"Not a project. I need your help with a meeting."

"Okay. I'll see what I can do. Who?"

"Nikhil King. I need to see Nik as soon as possible."

CHAPTER ELEVEN

DANIKA

"Jay, when I said arrange a meeting, you could have told me it was at a fight night," I stated to Jayna as I stared at the massive crowd of people surrounding a cage in the center of a giant warehouse.

The air was heated from the packed room, a sharp contrast from the cold outside. Shouts and groans echoed all around me.

When we'd driven into my old neighborhood, a wave of anxiety I hadn't expected coursed through my stomach. This was the first time in fifteen years I'd dared to step foot in my old world.

And even back in the day, the warehouse area was off-limits.

"Stupidity gets you killed or raped," Nik had warned me more times than I could remember.

Now here I was, with Jayna leading the way.

Thank God Jayna and my security had the good sense to lose the tail Uncle Ashok had assigned to us and believed we weren't aware of. Any news of this to him would complicate things in my life more than they already were.

"You wanted to meet Nik ASAP. Well, this is where he is tonight."

"Jay, I may have moved out of the area, but even I know this part of the hood is off- limits. It's not safe."

People cheered and yelled at whatever they were seeing inside the cage. I was too damn short to see clearly but it was obvious there was some sort of an epic match going on.

The walls of the room were covered in framed posters of famous boxers and pictures of local fighters. A few of them I recognized as being those of Nik's and Kir's birth fathers. It was amazing how much their sons looked like them.

"This is probably the safest place for either of us." Jayna weaved through the crowd of people, pulling me along behind her. "Anyone who even thinks about messing with us will have their heads crushed."

I stared at her in disbelief. "Something tells me you've been here quite a few times."

Jayna glanced over her shoulder and rolled her eyes. "Duh. How do you think Kiran and I met in the first place?"

Jayna had always had a rebellious streak because of Uncle Ashok's controlling nature. It was a game to see every-thing she could get away with. The last place I thought she'd venture to was this part of town.

"You said that you met at a club."

"I didn't lie. We met here. An underground fight club."

I gaped at her. "I feel like I don't even know you. I thought we shared everything."

"Don't act all hurt. I know you have some secrets of your own. Besides, I did tell you I met him at a club and it's true. I just didn't go into the details of what kind of club it was. We did end the night at a dance club, so I didn't really lie."

A large bald man covered in tattoos and a heavy beard

stepped in front of Jayna and then after some silent communication, he pointed to the cage.

Jayna stood on tiptoes and kissed his cheek and the giant man blushed.

"Come on, we will watch from there. Nik won't be free until after the fight."

"I guess you're a regular."

She nodded to different groups of people as she walked deeper toward the center of the room. "You could say that. I technically inherited it from Kir. This is his place. The guys run it for me."

By guys, I knew she meant the King brothers, Nikhil, Samir, and Reyhan.

God, how long had it been since I was in a room with all of them?

A wave of guilt burned in the pit of my stomach. I'd left and never looked back.

No, that wasn't true, I thought of them more often than not. Then, when they'd come up in the world as real estate developers, I consumed anything and everything about them in the papers, news, and gossip blogs. Especially anything to do with Nik, who the journalists loved to write about. His rags-to-riches story mixed with his unapologetic frankness about his past made for great reports.

"You're truly an enigma, Jay."

She snorted. "Takes one to know one."

She held my hand as we weaved through the masses of bodies. I couldn't help but notice the moment people saw Jayna, they stopped and cleared a path for her to get through.

Holy shit. She was like their queen.

I stared at her back. She probably had no clue about the

way people reacted to her. Jayna was single-minded in everything she did, especially driving Uncle Ashok nuts.

All thoughts of Jayna's antics disappeared the second the men fighting in the chain-link- fenced ring came into view.

Well, one in particular.

Hill. No, Nik.

I swallowed. This wasn't the polished gentleman from last night. This was the untamed, lethal man the boy I'd known had grown into.

Sweat glistened over his golden skin, and the muscles of his ripped, tattooed body bunched and flexed with his movements. His gray shorts hung from a sculpted waist. As he pivoted, I noticed a distinct scar that ran in a long gash on his back. A scar he'd gotten while trying to protect me from a local bully with a switchblade.

Why hadn't I noticed it last night?

Probably because I was too busy ogling his cock.

He kept his taped fists up as he shifted from one foot to the other. Nik's opponent gasped for air and mimicked Nik's stance. The two men were equally matched in height and build but there was no doubt Nik was the more dangerous of the two.

People all around me shouted, "Finish him!"

"In the stomach!"

"Kick his ass, King!"

Nik jabbed twice and jumped back as his opponent countered. Nik's gaze lifted for a blink of an eye and I immediately knew he saw me. He'd always had this way of knowing where I was.

My pulse jumped, and an ache throbbed deep in my core. The need for him hadn't calmed since I'd left him, and now it was raging.

Dammit. This was not the time to let my attraction for

Nikhil King come to the forefront. It was better to let it stay locked away. I was here for business. To stick it to Ashok Shah.

Thoughts of my dipshit uncle cooled my body and I focused on the fight again. For the next few minutes, the men in the cage punched, hit, and blocked, tracking all over the ring.

Then, as quickly as Talia had taken the gun out of my hand, Nik had his opponent sprawled on the floor with a strategic targeted punch to the abdomen.

The bell rang and cheers boomed all around me.

Jayna touched my hand and shouted, "Stay here. Nik is coming. I'll be back in a minute."

"What? You're leaving me here?"

There was no response as she disappeared into the horde of bodies.

"Fucking great," I muttered to myself.

The invisible barrier that was around me and Jayna evaporated as she left and people moved in, surrounding me.

This was one of those times I really hated being so damn short. Hell, at five-foot-one, I wasn't just short, I was microscopic compared to the giants in this warehouse.

Coming in here was a bad idea. I should go wait by the car.

Glancing over my shoulder, I spotted the exit. I could make it there. It wasn't too far.

Pushing and sliding between people, I made my way toward a nearby wall and then followed it toward the open doors.

Just as I felt the relief of freedom from the swarm of people, a large arm blocked my way and a giant body caged me against the wall.

"You weren't trying to sneak out of here without saying hello, were you, Danika?"

NIK

"Hill…Nik." Danika's face flushed as if caught by the big bad wolf, and then the calm she always wore locked into place.

I couldn't pretend that my name spoken through Danika's breathy voice wasn't something I'd wanted to hear for far too long. Even if she tried to pretend, she hadn't stopped herself from calling me by the name she'd given me as a frightened eight-year-old.

Now in less than twenty-four hours she'd used it multiple times.

I leaned closer to her ear. "You didn't answer my question."

Goddamn she smelled amazing—jasmine and spice.

"Hello, Nik. I'm sorry I can't stay." She tried to duck under my arm but I shifted too fast, blocking her.

"Of course, you can. We have a meeting scheduled, after all."

"I don't think this is a good time to talk. You seem busy." She kept her gaze toward the exit of the club.

"You can look at me. I'm not going to bite. Well, not unless you want me to."

Her breath caught, and her mask faltered again.

What would it be like to have this woman stand before me without any of the walls she loved to erect? Hell, I'd love to just have her the way she was last night, panting, desperate for my touch, for my cock, for me.

"Look at me, Danika."

"That's impossible with you blocking my movement." And we were back to the in-control woman she liked to show the world.

I dropped my arm and stepped back. She turned to study me. The way her beautiful hazel eyes scanned my body was almost like a physical caress.

After a few moments, she said, "I wanted to discuss the business proposition and terms I was going to bring to you on Wednesday."

"I figured as much when Jayna left a message telling me she was bringing you here tonight for a discussion."

Jayna coming to the club wasn't anything new. She'd pop in on occasion and watch a fight. She'd sit alone in one of the private balconies and then leave without a word to Sam, Rey, or me.

My brothers and I knew it was a way for her to feel close to Kiran. Especially since he was the one who'd started this club.

The fact Jayna had decided to bring Danika was something I hadn't expected. It would have been better for Danika and me to meet in my office, where I was in a suit and not shirtless, dripping in sweat, and starting to show the first signs of bruises.

But then again, Danika Dayal had seen me when I was a street rat without a penny to my name and an aunt who was too exhausted from working like a dog to keep an eye on me.

"Maybe talking right now isn't a good idea. We should meet in your office. Is there any way for you to fit me in tomorrow?"

She scanned me again, her gaze lingering on my abs before moving up to my face.

"Right now is the perfect time. Follow me."

Instead of waiting for a response, I turned and headed in the direction of the storeroom my brothers and I used as the club offices.

"You're still bossy as ever," she muttered under her breath, and I couldn't help but smile at her annoyance.

She'd always hated when I ordered her about. It never kept her from listening so it couldn't have been as irritating as she made it out to be.

"I'm who I am." I opened the metal door and then closed and locked it once she entered.

The sound of the latch made her jump, and all I could do was shake my head.

"Do I make you nervous?"

I grabbed a towel from a basket of clean ones and wiped the sweat from my face and body.

"No. I can't say you do." Danika's eyes darkened and my cock jumped.

Shit. This was not the time to get an erection. My shorts wouldn't hide a single inch of it.

I quickly moved to a fridge in the corner and pulled out two waters, tossing one to Danika.

Unscrewing the top, I drank the water down and then asked, "What was so urgent that you had to meet today?"

She clutched the plastic as she scanned me from head to shoes and then back up, lingering at the very place I'd rather she kept her attention away from.

"I…wanted…" She swallowed. "I have a…"

"Danika."

"Yes."

"If you keep looking at me like that, my control is going to snap and you'll be on your knees."

Instead of averting her gaze from my cock, she licked her lips.

Maybe it was the adrenaline still pumping through my system or the presence of this woman, without thinking I stalked in her direction, throwing my empty bottle on the floor. I cupped her jaw and throat with my palm, bringing my sweat-covered face an inch from hers and using my other hand to push her against the metal door.

"Don't. I've wanted to fuck you for too long and after last night, you're too tempting and I'm on the edge."

Her pupils dilated, the amber swallowed by black, leaving a golden ring. "You should know by now that the edge is where I like it."

"Is that right?"

"Yes." Her voice was breathy just as it had been only hours earlier.

She shifted, letting her abdomen rub my erection. Precum wept from the tip, and at this point I couldn't give a fuck if she noticed. It was her fault I was in this state.

"Then, you're about to play on it. And this time, I'll be the only one who comes."

Lifting her, I carried her to the desk in the back corner of the room.

"Nik—" she clutched my damp shoulders, "—we can't. Jayna will come looking for us."

"That doesn't sound like a real protest to me. Besides, you're the one who threw down the gauntlet."

Once I had her positioned on the desk, I tugged her jacket off and set her hands at the metal trim. "Hold it. And no matter what I do or who knocks on the door, do not move your fingers. No one can come in. The door is locked from the inside."

Her panted breaths were music to my ears.

"Do you understand?"

She nodded.

"Give me the words."

Licking her lips, she whispered, "Yes. I understand."

I set my bruised hands on her waist and slowly pushed her flimsy tank top up, taking my time to mold my fingers over her curves and up to her amazing tits. Once I had the shirt bunched over her breasts, I tugged the cups of her lace bra down, exposing her dark, hard nipples.

I wanted to suck the beautiful pebbles until she cried out. By the time she left this warehouse, she was going to need me so desperately that when she finally got down to business, it would take all her energy to focus on the subject she was presenting.

I was an asshole. I knew it. But I wasn't ashamed to admit I'd do what I needed to keep her.

She'd entered my world. Not just once but twice, and this one was where it was the rawest. Where the past never left. It melded with the present.

"Nik." A whimper escaped her mouth. "Stop staring at me like that. I ache."

Fuck.

Cupping her face, I moved in closer, letting my damp skin press against her soft, clean, feminine curves. "I'm not the polished man from last night. This is the raw street rat you left behind when you went off to your ivory tower."

Something flashed in her gaze before it disappeared. "A gilded cage is more accurate."

"One that you seem to navigate to your advantage."

"We all do what we have to in order to survive." Her attention shifted to my mouth as she leaned in.

"Very true. Are you ready?"

"Yes." She shifted closer and nipped my lower lip along the very spot where it swelled from a blow I'd taken during the fight. "I know who you are, Nik. Polished or not. Some things you don't ever forget."

Squeezing her jaw tighter, I kissed her hard. She growled as our tongues dueled for dominance, but the fact she hadn't moved her hands told me more than she would ever admit.

Pulling back, I stared into her desire-clouded eyes. "Then you should have known this thing between us would never have been just a onetime thing."

I stepped back and then shifted her so her elbows lay on the desk and her back and breasts were bowed up as if they were an offering.

This woman was a complete contradiction. One second, she was all business and bossy as hell and the next pliant and accommodating.

"In fact, it's going to be an over-and-over-again thing."

"Stop talking, Nik. And pull out your cock."

And there she went all bossy again, and for some reason it got me harder. Maybe it was the fact that no one ever pushed back with me, or because it was Danika.

There was no point questioning it.

Pushing my shorts down, my dick slapped against my stomach. I was so ready for her that my arousal splattered my abdomen.

She licked her lips as she watched me grab the base and squeeze.

A low whimper came from her and I had visions of her deep-throating me, of me teaching her the exact way I liked a woman's touch, of me coming down her mouth, of her swallowing every last drop of my cum.

How the fuck had she gone from an untouchable fantasy to a woman I had the pleasure of commanding in a matter of days?

It was going to be the rest of our lives soon enough.

"Set your heels on the edge of the desk and spread your legs apart."

"Nik. I…"

"Do it," I ordered, cutting off anything else she had to say.

She followed my command.

"Now slide your hand into your pants and stroke your pussy. I want you to show me what you do to yourself as you are thinking of me."

Her eyes widened as if I'd caught on to another of her secrets. After a few seconds, she complied, leveraging her body weight onto one forearm while she glided her fingers down her stomach, past the waistband of her pants, and between the folds of her pussy lips.

She closed her eyes, losing herself in the pleasure she gave herself.

That was until I said, "Don't you want to watch the show in front of you?"

Her lids snapped open.

She watched me stroke my cock up and down, finding the rhythm I liked. What she probably didn't realize was that having her here laid out as my personal pinup girl was the ultimate fantasy come to life.

She worked her pussy under her clothes with each pass of my cock, her breathing growing faster and harder.

She bit her lip, a whimper of need escaping her mouth. Abruptly she pulled free of her pants and readied to jump off the desk.

"Nik, please. Let me suck you."

God, I wanted nothing more, but not this time.

"No. Stay right there. You said you liked the edge. Well, this is an edge, Danika." I continued to pump my cock as my balls drew up.

Her nails scored the wood, and I'd never forget how the marks got there, or the arousal covering the fingers she'd pulled free of her body before marking the table.

"I need to do something." There was a desperation to her movements as she cupped her bare breasts.

"You want to do something? Offer me your tits. I'm going to come all over them."

"But I want…"

"Take it or leave it."

She shifted forward, doing as I'd said. She really was a fucking goddess.

I couldn't hold out anymore. Everything inside me tightened.

"Fuck," I called out as my cum shot out, covering her heaving breasts in heavy ropes.

By the time I pumped the last of my orgasm free, Danika's golden skin was a gorgeous canvas. There was something primal about marking her in this way.

Some may think I'm a sick fuck but I couldn't give a damn.

I'd claimed her. Deep down, she knew it. Soon, I'd make it crystal clear.

CHAPTER TWELVE

DANIKA

I held my cum-covered breast, panting and not believing I'd let myself fall under Nik King's spell.

Again.

My body needed release and I was ready to beg for him to give it to me.

What was wrong with me? Damn Nik and his magic cock.

And the sad part was I hadn't even had his cock yet. What would happen when I actually slept with him?

I wasn't going to lie to myself and pretend it wasn't going to happen. I was drawn to him like no other man. And now that I'd opened the forbidden door, Nik would never let me close it again.

"Do you have any idea how beautiful you are?"

Our eyes connected.

"This isn't why I came here."

"I know. We will get to that later." He stepped closer, swiping a finger through the cum cooling on my skin and then bringing it to my lips. "Open."

I'd wanted to taste him; here was my chance. I opened

my mouth and then closed it around his long finger, letting my teeth graze his skin as he pulled free.

His slightly salty, sweet essence filled my taste buds and I hummed.

Fire lit his dark eyes. "Now you are well and truly marked, Danika Dayal. Inside and out."

His words sent a shiver down my spine "What the hell does that mean?"

"It means, you're mine."

"I told you this last night. I belong to no man."

He gripped the back of my head, pulling me against him and not caring that he was smearing his cum all over us. He kissed me with a savage intensity I hadn't experienced yet and I found myself responding to it and wrapping my legs around his naked waist. His cock was thick and long between us, adding to the unfulfilled need brewing throughout me.

Drawing back, he dropped his forehead to mine and said, "I'm not fucking you here. It's not the time or the place for it."

"There doesn't seem to be a convenient time or place for us. Maybe the universe is telling us something."

He lifted his head. "Rest assured, Danika, it's going to happen. But after this meeting of ours. After our business dealings. After you completely understand the price for the favor I am going to do for you."

"I said business, not a favor."

"It's all the same in my world."

"You can't intimidate me, Nik."

He captured my wrists and held them against the hollow of my back. A shiver went down my spine.

"Are you sure about that? You're shaking."

"Shaking from wanting to fuck you is vastly different than being afraid of you."

"Glad you understand the difference." He smiled. "Then what should I ask as my payment?"

"Something reasonable."

"I don't do reasonable. My favors come at a price, and usually I collect what is most valuable to a person. What is most valuable to you Danika?"

My freedom.

"You don't have to tell me what it is right now. Just decide if you are willing to give it to me for whatever it is you need me to do for you."

I twisted my hands in a motion that loosened his grip and set my hand on his chest. "What I'm going to offer you is more than enough compensation for what I want from you."

"As I told you last night, I'll take what you're offering and will expect more. I'm the ruler of this empire. I make the rules."

"And how does this—" I gestured between us, "—play into the bargain?"

"I won't lie. Some things will overlap, but for the most part, what happens between us is all about us."

At least he wasn't giving me some bullshit.

"You make it sound as if this is going to be more than casual."

"With our history, it was never going to be casual. You're lying to yourself if you believe otherwise."

"More between us isn't possible. I have plans that a relationship will complicate." I slipped under his arms and off the table. "I'll come by your office tomorrow morning. I'm sure you can fit me in."

I grabbed a towel from a nearby basket to wipe the cooling cum from my chest.

Fuck. My shirt was trashed. Glancing around the room, I found a stack of folded T-shirts in another basket. Pulling my shirt over my head, I tossed it in the garbage before taking a clean one from the pile and slipping it on.

The damn thing was too big. I gathered and tied it on the side. This would have to do.

I glanced at my watch. Jayna was probably looking for me. Quickly grabbing and shrugging on the jacket that had fallen to the floor, I moved to the metal door, but Nik blocked my way.

He'd slipped on a shirt of his own as well as a pair of shorts. "You walked back into my world. You complicated things. Now you will deal with the consequences."

The tone of his voice had a tinge of something that brought back so many memories and made me want to cup his face and kiss him.

"I was fourteen when I left. It wasn't as if I had a choice."

"And I let you live a life without my existence."

"We aren't children anymore."

"That's right. We're adults, making choices based on the demons of our past."

I narrowed my eyes. "What do you know of it?"

"I know you hate Ashok Shah and will do anything to get back at him." I stared at him, not saying a word.

"Deny it."

"I can't. But there is something you have wrong. I don't just want to get back at him. I plan to take everything from him as he did from my parents, Jayna, me, and Samir."

Nik gave away no reaction, just held my gaze. "And you plan to make this happen with my help?"

"No, with something you either have or can get me."

"And are you willing to pay my price?"

"If it means Ashok Shah goes down in an epic explosion of flames, then I say yes."

"And if I say the price is you?"

I swallowed. "Me? What does that mean?"

"I'm saying is your wrath, your vengeance, your revenge worth giving me you...body, mind, and soul?"

"You make it sound as if you're the devil, who will make my dreams come true if only I sell him my soul."

"Some people believe I am the devil." He ran a thumb over my lower lip. "Think on the answer very hard. The price is going to tie you to me for eternity."

"Nik, I won't let you scare me."

"I should scare you. I let our history push us back into familiar roles, but you need to understand who you're playing with. I'm not that seventeen-year-old you left behind. I'm everything the rumors say. I'm not nice, I'm not sweet, and I will take and use until I'm satisfied."

I knew that was bullshit. Why was he flipping on me like this? What was the point of this one-eighty?

"When you get home, honestly answer these questions. What would it take for you to give up this quest? Is there anyone or anything more important than destroying Shah? If the answer is no, then come to my office and we'll do business tomorrow at eight. Otherwise, we will keep it personal and forget about business."

"I won't change my mind." He was not going to confuse me or have me second-guessing my decisions.

"Then I guess I'll see you tomorrow at eight."

"No, I want this settled tonight."

NIK

I couldn't believe she was determined to talk business after what just happened between us. After I'd all but tried to scare her shitless with what I'd expect of her.

"Tomorrow, Danika." I leaned forward, this time using my size to crowd her against the metal door of the office.

She lifted her face to mine, a crease forming between her brows. "Tonight."

"This isn't the place for negotiations. Especially not with the smell of sex in the air."

A slight flush tinged her cheeks, but she kept any other reaction schooled away. "It doesn't bother me. Especially since you already implied sex between us is a given even if it isn't part of the bargain."

"Fine." My hands lowered to grip her hips, harder than I intended, but I was frustrated beyond anything I ever experienced with any other woman. "What is it you want from me?"

"I want what you have on my uncle."

"What makes you think I have anything on him?"

She clenched her teeth. "Because he wanted me to whore myself out to you in order to get it."

"Say that again."

Shah wouldn't actually expect Danika to fuck me to get the will. Then again, I couldn't put anything past the man. His own personal gain always came before anything.

"You heard me. Apparently, we haven't done a very good job of hiding our attraction, and therefore he believes my pussy has the power to charm you into giving me this information or item. I want it. Not for him. But for me."

"And what exactly do you think it is?"

She held my gaze. "My *Ma*'s will."

I couldn't help but smile. This woman's intelligence was beyond scary. She knew the only thing that would keep Shah in line was a threat to his empire, and Sara Shah's will was the key.

"And let's say I have it. What makes you think I will give you my leverage on Shah?"

"Because the will is the key to fucking up his perfect life."

"I want to know, exactly what do you plan to do with this will?"

"Before I give you any details and this discussion goes any further, I need to know if you have it."

"I have a copy. Not the original."

I wouldn't lie to her.

A flash of disappointment crossed her face. "Does it have the signatures?"

"Yes, I authenticated your grandmother's signature against other documents filed in public record."

"And who owns everything?"

"You know that answer, Danika. Now we are at the point where we discuss the price for this expensive favor you need."

She set a hand on my chest and pushed me back, moving out of my arms and over to the desk where I'd had her splayed out only moments ago.

"If I'm going into debt, might as well go all in. I have more favors, as you put it. And in return, I will make it so no one will ever be able to hack your enterprise again."

"What makes you think I have any issues with hacking? Rey is more than capable of handling anything."

She smirked. "I have two words for you: messy desktop."

So, this was the mysterious hacker who left packaged files on properties and developments on my computer. Rey had gone through every channel he knew to trace the culprit only to end up lost in a loop of servers all over the world.

Why hadn't I guessed? I knew her secret. I knew her

skills. I shouldn't have put it past her to hack my network to give me information that would fuck up an investment for her uncle.

I had to see how far she was going to play this card. "Who do you work for?"

"Jayna. I'm an art appraiser." There was a smirk on her face.

She was fucking with me. "Danika," I warned.

"I'm what you call a freelancer."

"And your relationship with Devani Patel?"

A crease formed between her brows. "That information is not part of this negotiation. Back to favors. Here are my terms."

"I'm listening." I folded my arms and leaned against the door.

"In addition to the copy of the will, I want you to acquire the wooden chest my mother carved and the letters she wrote me before her death."

"Say that again."

"You couldn't have forgotten. I told you about the letters and the chest. Uncle Ashok was supposed to give me them when I was sixteen and has never given them to me. I want them."

The fucker was something else. Whatever he had, it wasn't the chest.

"What else?"

"When the time comes to use the will against my uncle, you will back me to oust him from the board and the company. I know you bought a large percentage of shares when Shah International went public."

"How do you know this?"

She lifted a brow as if I'd asked a stupid question.

"Is that the last of the favors you require of me?"

She nodded. "Yes."

I slowly moved in her direction. "Now that you've stated your favors, I have a few conditions in addition to your technological skills."

She braced her hands on the desk. "Let me hear them."

"First, you will let Shah believe that you're following through with his plan. You will play the dutiful niece, ask for forgiveness for the temper I'm sure you showed him when he sprung his request on you, and remain close to him."

"No," she spat. "I will not let him believe I'm his to whore out, whether you and I are sleeping together or not."

"I wouldn't tell you to do it if I didn't have a reason. I need you to find every bit of information he has hidden about Kir's accident. The only way to search his office is to be close to him."

"I knew you never believed the bullshit about Kir's death."

"So, you searched for the truth?"

"Yes, I searched every place I could think of, including hacking every server associated with him, his companies, or any of his known associates. There's no trace of his involvement."

I should have figured she would have looked into this. Her relationship with Kir was beyond that of cousin-in-law; he was a surrogate brother. She would have done everything possible to find out the truth. Shah wasn't a stupid man. He wouldn't have used resources that could trace back to him—nothing with an electronic footprint, anyway.

"Did you search his home office?"

She looked away. "No. That is the only place I have never gotten access to investigate. He has that place under constant surveillance. He doesn't trust anyone alone in there, not even the cleaning staff. The only time I'm allowed in there is if he arranges a meeting."

"You will have your opportunity in exactly two months. He is planning a large event on his estate."

She cocked her head to the side. "What's happening then?"

"Your uncle is announcing his candidacy to the senate."

"Bullshit."

It was my turn to lift a brow. "Believe what you will. On the night of that event, you will search his office and find the evidence I need to prove he was behind Kir's accident."

She swallowed. "Anything else?"

"Yes. One more thing. This is where business and personal would overlap."

"What is that?"

I leaned forward, until my lips were a fraction away from hers. "You're going to marry me."

"What?" She drew back, her fingers digging into the metal of the desk.

I set my hands on her waist. "You heard me."

"You don't want to marry me. You can't." There was fear and panic in her words.

"I do."

"Why would you want to marry me?" She pushed at my chest but couldn't move me, then she fisted my shirt.

"Those reasons are mine. These are my terms. You want to take down Ashok Shah, then you agree to become a King."

"Nik."

"Danika."

"Don't do this," she whispered. "There would be consequences to both of us."

"I asked you if Shah's destruction was worth giving me

you…body, mind, and soul. You answered yes. What did you think this encompassed? I told you I will take more than you are willing to give."

"Let's say I agreed to your terms. How will this play out with our plan for my uncle?"

"Those details we can work out at a later time. Neither of us will do anything that will complicate the other's plans."

"Marriage is the biggest complication a couple can enter."

"From where I'm looking, it's the simplest."

"How is that?"

"It makes it clear to everyone that you belong to me. Especially you."

Before I could respond, there was a bang on the door. The metal vibrated like an alarm, breaking the sexually charged tension growing between us.

I stepped back, inhaling deep. I knew we should have waited until tomorrow to discuss this. Now she was going to run.

I called out, "Yes."

"It's me, Jay. Is Dani with you?"

I glanced at her. She was still pressed to the desk.

"I'm here." Danika kept her gaze on my face. "Nik and I are in the middle of a discussion."

"Well, hurry it up. I'm ready to go home."

"What's your answer, Danika?"

"Where will we live? I have a life. I…" She trailed off.

"We will start off this coming Friday at my place and figure it out from there. First I need a yes."

Her hazel eyes filled as if she was about to cry then calmed, and she stood up and stepped into my space. "My answer is yes. But you may regret it, Nikhil King."

"When it comes to you, I've never had any regrets." I

threaded my fingers in her hair and pulled her in for one last kiss before releasing her.

She moved toward the metal door, unlocking it and pulling it open.

Jayna looked between Danika and me for a few seconds before a smile tugged at her lips.

Fuck. That woman was too perceptive. There was no way to hide the tension between Danika and me.

"Let's go." Danika moved out of the office but paused, glancing over her shoulder. "I'll see you at our appointment."

CHAPTER THIRTEEN

NIK

I watched the security monitors as Jayna and Danika climbed into their car. The two guards who'd waited outside the club weren't the ones we'd assigned to Jayna, but Danika's. They shared the same lethal edge my men carried with the added benefit of polish and refinement, which only meant they were trained by Rich Kade and the best.

I couldn't fault the man for watching out for Danika. He had a need to protect her as much as I did.

The woman who'd stood before me tonight had given me flashes of the girl I'd known long ago.

The one with big expressive eyes and a heart too innocent for the neighborhood we lived in. The girl who'd all but turned my life upside down, who'd talked to me as if I was a real person, instead of the street rat I knew I was.

She'd been an enigma back then and it seemed she still was.

Soon, I'd unravel the puzzle, but first I had to make sure Shah never found out about this visit.

I sent a quick text to my team verifying no one followed

the two women and had Jayna's driver make a few detours before dropping the girls off.

More than likely Danika had it under control, but it wouldn't hurt to provide extra precautions.

Setting my phone down, I braced my arms on the table. The adrenalin from the fight, the mind-blowing orgasm, and crazy-as-fuck negotiation had left me in need of a fifth of scotch straight.

Get it together, King. You're not that idiot teen boy anymore. You got what you wanted, now live with it.

I glanced to my side and stared at the wall where my brothers and I kept pictures of most of our birth parents.

What would those humble people think of what became of us?

They'd died too young to guide us in life, only able to pass on a few lessons to get by on and the barest of traditions of their blending of cultures.

Sitting on top of their pictures sat Arin's.

I'd never be able to repay him for saving us the way he had.

I moved over to the wall and touched the picture of a beautiful Afro-Trinidadian woman, with her head resting against the side of a large man, who dwarfed her in size. His gaze was on his wife, and there was a look of awe as he watched her.

There was no doubt Haresh and Lisa Guru had cared for each other. They'd given up family fortunes and social standing in a life in Trinidad for one together in the United States.

From the stories Aunt Beverly told me, both of them had come from affluent families who wanted their children to marry within their individual communities. My mother's being Afro-Trinidadian and my father's being Indian. They'd met at a city festival and then secretly started seeing each other, knowing neither of their families would approve. When their relationship was discovered, instead of trying to convince both sets of parents to accept them, which they knew wasn't possible, they decided to move out of the Caribbean and settle in New York.

Not ten years later, when I was barely nine, they were killed in a bus crash on their way home from the metal factory they worked in. A crash that had also killed Kir's and Rey's parents and Sam's mother.

It was the first of many tragedies that went beyond blood and bonded us as brothers. And maybe it was part of what drew me to Danika. Her story wasn't any better, even if she lived in the world of affluence, art, and designer clothes.

My phone rang, drawing my attention away from the picture.

Walking back to the table, I picked up the mobile, read the display, and then answered, "What can I do for you, Commissioner Travis?"

"Your situation with the development permits is cleared. You can proceed as planned."

"Thank you. As agreed, your brother's crew will start work in the next few weeks."

"Does this mean we're even?"

"For this instance. On my count, we still have two more on the tally sheet."

"Any idea when you plan to collect on them?"

"Not as of yet, but you'll be the first to know. Have a good evening, Commissioner." I hung up and smiled.

Soon construction of a community center would begin right in front of the property where Shah planned to put up the newest of his hotels, making it useless for any grand-scale development. With a community center in progress, Shah would find it all but impossible to have zoning changed for his project.

And this would never have been possible if it wasn't for the tip from Danika.

Damn woman had hacked me.

I could still see the smug expression on her face when she'd said, "Messy desktop."

The fact it made me hard just thinking about her abilities meant I was probably going to spend the rest of my life covering up an erection whenever she was around.

"What the hell was that?" Sam asked as he stalked into the club office. "I thought we agreed to keep Dani safe. When the fuck did you two become so chummy?"

"She sought me out and I just let things play out."

Sam clenched his jaw. "What does she want?"

"Let's wait until Rey gets here so I don't have to repeat myself."

"You're such an asshole."

"I never denied this."

Sam glared at me. "I will beat your ass if you put her in the middle of this thing with Shah."

"Get in line." I shrugged. "Kir already warned me off. And as I told him, I'm playing the cards I was dealt."

"What the fuck does that mean?" His gaze went to the garbage can and shirt hanging off the edge. "You moth-erfucker."

He charged for me. I braced for impact, but Rey grabbed Sam.

"What the fuck, man?" Rey threw Sam onto the couch. "Calm down."

Even though I was a good fifty pounds heavier than Sam, we were a good match when it came to a fight. I was built like a boxer, whereas he was all street fighter, lean and muscled. Rey, on the other hand, was a combination of both of us, he had the skills of a heavyweight boxer and mixed martial artist. He'd kick all of our asses. The only one of us who could have ever challenged him back in the day was Kir.

"He's fucking Dani."

Rey's head whipped in my direction. "You're what?"

"If the two of you settle down, I will give you the details. And before you try to bash my head in, and I mean try—because we know it's not going to happen—Danika and I are engaged."

Sam lunged for me again, but Rey set his foot on his stomach and pushed him down. "Sit down, asshole."

I moved to the refrigerator, grabbed three beers, and handed them to the guys. Popping the top to mine, I chugged it down and then released a deep breath.

"Danika wants the information on Shah, specifically the copy of the will."

"We can't give it to her. She doesn't know the hell that will break free if we do." The edge in Sam's voice said he'd protect the family he'd never been able to claim no matter the cost. "She isn't one to sit on it. She'll throw it in Shah's face and then he'll retaliate."

"Do you really think I'd put her in danger?"

Sam shook his head. "No."

"Before I get into it, want to tell me why you kept the fact that Danika and Ms. Patel are regulars at The Library from me?"

"Nope. I don't question your decisions when it comes to your role in the organization, you don't need to question mine."

I clenched my jaw. "And you know they're in business together?"

"Yes. Unlike you, I follow the rules of our establishment.

The information I learn there, stays there. Now get on with it."

"And you call me the asshole." I ran a hand over my face. "Danika wants revenge on Shah. She knows he took her inheritance. She wants to take back everything owed to her, including what is owed to Jayna and you."

I looked directly at Sam.

He narrowed his gaze. "She knows how I feel on the matter."

"That seems to be irrelevant. Whether you accept your portion or not, she's determined to get the company."

Before Sam could make another comment, I continued, "There are a few other things you both need to know."

Rey leaned forward. "We're listening."

"Shah wants the will. He wants Danika to seduce me and believes if she sleeps with me, I'll let her drag me around by my dick and eventually give her the will."

"As if Danika is just going to hand over a document that says she owns all of Shah International."

"Technically, it says you and Jayna own it too."

"I don't want it."

"It's yours whether you touch it or not."

"And did you agree to give it to her?"

"Yes."

"At what cost?" There was anger radiating from Sam, and Rey all but sat on him to keep him in place.

"Sex wasn't part of the agreement, but marriage was. If you ever believed Danika and I weren't inevitable then I'm calling you a liar. She walked into The Library and it happened. Now to the agreement.

"For the will and my support when she takes over the board, she will marry me and she will get the evidence we need to prove Shah was behind Kir's wreck.'"

CHAPTER FOURTEEN

DANIKA

A little after eight on Saturday morning, I handed Rich my suitcase and slid into the back seat of my car.

He looked at the bag and then back at me. "Where to, Dani?"

My stomach clenched in knots. "To Nikhil King's building."

Rich studied me as if asking, "What are you doing? And why don't I know about it?"

"He is the only one who can make things change," I explained, even though Rich hadn't really asked anything.

I licked my parched lips, wanting to look away, but I held his gaze.

Rich deserved to know what I planned, but I knew he'd try to talk me out of it.

"I will stay in the area, in case you change your mind and decide to go home."

"No." I shook my head. "You can go home after I go inside. One of his men will bring my things. I'll call you Monday when I'm ready for work."

After a few more seconds of staring at me, he nodded, not hiding the concern in his green eyes.

He closed the door, set my suitcase in the trunk, and moved into the driver's seat.

As we slid into traffic, I gazed out of the window, watching cars, taxis, and pedestrians, but not really seeing them.

In less than an hour, my life would change beyond anything I'd expected. I was really going to do this.

I had to accept it.

I wanted to take down Uncle Ashok, and this was the price. God, I still couldn't believe he wanted to marry me.

Marriage wasn't part of any plan I'd had for my life. Well, not unless I had a love that was as close as possible to the one my parents had shared.

Their love was almost out of a fairytale, but it hadn't had the storybook ending I wished it had.

My mom, Reka, was raised with the expectation of an arranged marriage to a wealthy businessman who ran in the same circles as she was raised in. Instead, she'd met Kris Dayal, a lowly desk clerk, who worked in one of her family's hotels and could barely afford to pay his rent as he worked his way through engineering school.

In the beginning, they'd kept a friendly relationship with nothing more than a casual greeting whenever they encountered each other. Then one day, while trying to escape an argument with Uncle Ashok about accepting a marriage proposal, Mummy and Papa ran into each other at a bar where local college kids hung out. Papa had offered to help Mama take her mind off her family troubles and showed her New York City from the perspective of those without privilege.

A real friendship developed that night and soon Mama

met up with Papa multiple times a week. Eventually, they realized they were in love. Around the same time, Uncle Ashok found out Mummy was sneaking out to meet Papa.

Immediately he fired Papa from his clerk job and came down hard on Mummy, keeping her under constant watch and forcing her to only associate with people he approved.

It wasn't until one day when Mummy was out with *Ma*, my grandmother, that she found an escape from the oppressiveness of Uncle Ashok. *Ma* was a widow who'd had a love marriage, unlike many of the arranged marriages of her generation. She'd seen how unhappy Mummy was and decided to help her.

While they were shopping, *Ma* handed Mummy an envelope with money and some jewelry and told her to find her happiness. *Ma* would rather have Mummy living away from her than see her daughter so miserable.

Mummy and Papa married within the month and moved to the neighborhood where I was born. From what I knew, not once had she regretting giving up a life of opulence and privilege to be with Papa. And I had no doubt it was the truth. Our house was always filled with so much laughter and love.

Well, that was true until Mummy got sick.

The cancer came on quick and in a matter of months, she was gone. And then, a few years later, Papa was killed in a supposed random shooting, and as a result I was whisked into the life Mummy had escaped.

A life I'd never fit into nor wanted.

"We're here." Rich's voice broke into my thoughts. "Do you want me to escort you up?"

I spotted one of Nik's men, the one who shadowed Nik everywhere he went. The man moved toward the car, typing something on his phone.

"No."

"One call and I'll be back. I don't give a shit who he is. I will get you out."

I scooted forward in my seat and set a hand on Rich's shoulder. "I'll be fine. One thing you can be positive of is that Nik would never hurt me."

"I'll remain cautious for your sake. His man is approaching." Rich pressed the button to pop the trunk as my door opened.

A blast of cold February air engulfed me, making me shiver.

Slowly, I stepped out and found myself looking into sharp blue eyes. They were filled with an edge of humor and had none of the hardness I expected from anyone who worked for Nik.

"King is waiting for you." He gestured to the revolving door leading into the building.

I glanced one last time at Rich before walking toward the entrance of the brick building.

The second I stepped into the lobby, I was hit by the classic opulence of the room.

It was breathtaking, as if I'd time-traveled into early nineteen-hundreds New York. Drapes of deep blue colors hung over the oversized windows. Embroidered fabric-covered sofas sat on marble floors. And a brass-and-crystal chandelier bigger than most New Yorkers' apartments hung from a ceiling intricately painted in the same hues as the drapes.

I knew Nik owned the high rise and had renovated it, but this wasn't what I'd expected of him. I saw him in something modern, clean lined, and sparse.

Then again, I didn't know the man he'd become, just the

memories of the boy from long ago who never wanted anything old.

I stared up at the designs on the ceiling, completely in awe of the detail and beauty. Whoever Nik had hired to do the work must have cost a fortune. "This way, Ms. Dayal."

I stopped gawking and asked, "Are you taking me up?"

"No. According to Nik, you aren't the type to walk into the lion's den behind anyone. Well, unless it plays to your advantage."

Why would Nik share anything about me? That made no sense. The fact Nik had either meant this guy was more than just his bodyguard or that his organization wasn't run like anything I could understand.

It was probably both. So far nothing of my encounters with Nik made any sense.

"What's your name?"

A smile broke out on his face, completely softening the hardness from only moments before. "You don't remember me, do you?"

I studied him and then saw the resemblance to the little boy who'd keep me company on the steps of the corner shop whenever Nik wasn't around.

"Lake?"

He bowed. "At your service."

Without thinking, I stood on tiptoes and hugged him. His body stiffened for a second and then relaxed, but he kept his hands straight down.

"I've thought about you so many times over the years, wondering what happened to you."

Lake had been one of the sweetest kids I'd ever met. He'd been a lot like me, awkward, nerdy, with the exception of being on the larger side for his age. Something that hadn't changed. He had to be over six and a half feet tall and built like a wall. No wonder he was Nik's security.

As I stepped back, he adjusted his suit and said, "Nik happened."

Yes, Nik. He happened to a lot of people.

"Still reading?"

"Every chance I get." Lake pushed the elevator button and it immediately opened. "I'm sure we'll catch up later. He's waiting."

I inhaled deep and nodded, stepping into the cab. The short ride up gave me time to settle my nerves and ready myself for what I was about to do.

And the calm immediately disappeared the moment the doors opened and revealed Nik standing before me.

My pulse jumped and my core clenched.

Damn the man for looking so good.

The stubble on his jaw hardened the perfection of his face. Not to mention those dark eyes that saw way too much.

He was dressed in a black suit tailor-made for his fighter's body. The white button-down shirt he wore underneath had the collar open, revealing a small hint of the tattoos that snaked up his shoulder and behind his neck.

He should have looked refined, in the way any up-and-coming New York real estate mogul would look, but instead he oozed danger. The kind sensible women threw caution to the wind for just a little touch.

Hell, I wasn't just throwing caution to the wind, I was jumping into the storm, binding myself to him for "eternity," as he'd put it.

"Ready?" He scanned me from head to toes, not revealing any emotion. "The judge is waiting."

I swallowed and then nodded, following behind him as he moved into the penthouse.

Turning abruptly, he grabbed my waist, keeping me from stumbling into him. "One last chance to escape. Is taking down Shah worth marrying me?"

Something about the way he'd spoken made me think he hadn't believed I'd show up.

Why was he giving me an out? Even back in the day, he gave no one outs. Once a deal was struck, one paid up or lost everything.

"Yes." I lifted my chin. "I'm still the girl you knew as a teen, even if the outside is different. Once I make a decision, nothing will change my mind."

"And if I told you I'm not the same kid you knew?"

"You're right. The kid had to grow up."

"Then you understand there is no divorce. This is death do us part."

A chill went down my spine, but not in fear as it should have. Something in my gut told me this was probably the best decision for me. Besides, he was the only boy I ever imagined marrying, even if it had been an adolescent daydream.

Nik had a reputation for being ruthless and had a willingness to go to any lengths to protect those he claimed as his. He would never hurt me. I only hoped he had no regrets in the long run.

I wasn't the girl I projected to the world.

Who was I kidding? Nik always saw past every wall I'd erected to keep the world outside. Even when we barely spoke, one look told me he knew the game I played.

"And what happens if you want out?"

"I'm the last one to worry about. I've been all in since I gave you the name Little Rabbit."

My heart jumped.

Before I could respond to him, Nik grasped my purse, setting it on a table.

"Wait."

He frowned and watched me as I went to my bag, opened it, and then pulled out a velvet box.

"You bought me a ring?" There was surprise in his question that had me glad I'd thought to get him one.

I'd had a jeweler friend of mine bring over a selection of rings a few days ago. The one I'd picked was made of tungsten carbide dipped in platinum. Something that looked expensive and also was solid, hard, and virtually unbreakable at the core. Very much like the man before me.

"Yes. I assumed you expected me to wear one. It was only fitting for you to do the same."

"Thank you."

"You're welcome."

Nik guided me toward a man sitting in a wingback chair by the floor-to-ceiling windows. As we approached, he stood, adjusted his suit, and faced me.

He had a light tanned complexion and lines around his face that came with age, white hair speckled with black, and a genuine smile that reminded me of an indulgent grandfather.

"So, this is Danika. I've heard a lot about you over the years."

I glanced at Nik, who kept his gaze on the judge.

Why would he talk about me to anyone? First Lake and now the judge.

I offered the judge my hand. "I'm sorry to say I don't know anything about you."

When the judge released me, Nik took my hand, bringing me next to him.

"Judge Davis was Arin's personal counsel for nearly thirty years. Now he's shifted gears so he can order the riffraff of the world to behave themselves or risk going to jail."

A look passed between Nik and the judge. There was a lot more to their history than I knew. Maybe one day I'd learn the whole of it.

"Are the witnesses here?" Judge Davis asked as he moved into position in front of us.

A few seconds later, the elevator opened, Lake and Rich stepping out.

There was concern in Rich's stare that said we would talk later.

I hadn't told anyone about the terms of the deal Nik and I had struck. I knew if Rich had known marriage was part of the bargain, he would have definitely done everything to stop it.

He took his promise to Papa seriously. The fact he was here to stand up for me as a witness meant more to me than he knew.

"Let's get you two married." Judge Davis opened a black book and began the ceremony.

Over the course of the next twenty minutes, both Nik and I signed papers, said our vows, exchanged rings, and sealed everything with a kiss.

A kiss that was barely a brushing of mouths but hit me like a ton of bricks and lingered after we'd pulled apart.

"Congratulations," Judge Davis said. "You are officially man and wife. One day I want to officiate a proper wedding."

His words sounded more like an order than a request.

When I glanced at his face, he was staring at Nik, who nodded and said, "I hear you."

I really was missing something.

The judge turned to me. "I'll see you again soon. Next time, I'm going to pick your brain about some artwork I'm interested in."

His kind eyes and genuine smile released the tension in my stomach that I hadn't realized was there.

I set a hand on his arm and said, "You know where to find me."

"Now I will take my leave. I have a date with my wife." Judge Davis moved to the elevator, flanked by Lake and Rich.

They disappeared the second the doors closed, leaving Nik and me in his enormous living room alone.

Exhaling, I shuddered inside as I stared at my gorgeous pink and white diamond wedding band and let the enormity of what I'd just done hit me.

I'd married Nikhil King.

A former gang leader turned real estate developer. A man who dealt in favors for a price. A man who seemed to know me so well that he'd picked a ring I'd have chosen for myself. One that was simple enough to wear every day but large enough to draw the eye, giving no doubt I was taken.

I swallowed, trying to relieve my dry throat.

Glancing to my side, I found Nik leaning against the window, holding a glass of dark amber liquid and staring at me. I'd been so lost in thought that he'd had enough time to shuck his jacket and roll his shirt sleeves to his elbows.

"Regrets already?"

CHAPTER FIFTEEN

DANIKA

The intensity of Nik's gaze had my stomach clenching.

"No." I shook my head. "As I remember, you told me regrets are for the weak. I'm not weak."

He took a sip of his drink. "That's for sure, you're not. You wouldn't have survived Shah if you were."

I almost asked him what he knew about my time with Uncle Ashok, but held it back. This wasn't the time for those specific secrets.

Instead, I posed a question. "What now?"

"You tell me." He lifted a brow. "Business or pleasure?"

Goosebumps prickled my skin. The way he all but purred the end part had my pussy growing slick with unquenched need.

Now I was desperate for him and that pissed me off to no end.

So instead of caving to my body's needs, I asked for something I knew he couldn't possibly have in his possession so soon. "You have the letters?"

"I've always had them."

"What?" I braced my hand on a nearby table. "But then what does Uncle Ashok have?"

"Nothing. The box he has is a replica made from a picture."

My lips trembled. "Why do you have them?"

He looked away for a brief moment. "After you left, I broke into your old apartment, looking for anything to lure you back. I found the chest hidden in your dad's closet and took it. I assumed you'd come searching for it since you talked about it so much. But…"

"I never came back." I finished his sentence as I closed my eyes and let a tear slip down my cheek.

All these years, Nik had it. I could have gotten it from him, if only I'd asked or bothered to find out.

"This isn't the time for tears, Mrs. King." Nik cupped my face, lifting it to meet his gaze. "Let's leave business until the morning. I believe pleasure is what's on the menu."

He was right. I'd waited all these years. One more night wasn't going to hurt.

The softness in his dark eyes had my heart hammering. This was a Nik I hadn't experienced yet.

All these years of skirting each other with only the memories of our past between us, with nothing more than simple touches between us as teens. Now I was about to be consumed by the volcano that was Nikhil King.

He'd had a reputation as a ladies' man. Women threw themselves at him, knowing he'd never had anyone steady in his life and probably never would. A perpetual bachelor, the gossip blogs had called him.

Now, here we were. He was my husband.

A man who'd married me for reasons he wasn't going to

tell me. A man I'd married to take down my uncle, not for love.

We were using each other. A fucked-up foundation for a marriage, without a doubt.

But there was one thing I knew neither of us could deny.

Our attraction.

Sex would be the one thing clear between us. We'd have no secrets there. We wanted each other.

As teenagers, it was innocent. He was my adolescent crush. Then as the years passed, the physical desire between us grew. It was almost as if he was a forbidden chocolate I was desperate to get a small bite of but knew one taste wouldn't be enough.

"I agree. Tonight isn't for anything but pleasure."

He rubbed his thumb over my lower lip. "From this moment on, you're mine."

"And are you mine, Nik?"

"There is no other for either of us."

"Hill—"

He cut me off by pulling me toward him and sealing his mouth to mine. His lips were soft, softer than I expected, and he tasted so good.

Of scotch and orange peel. And Nik.

This was nothing like the simple peck he'd given me when we sealed our vows. It was all-consuming, intoxicating, as if he was branding me, claiming me, making it clear I was his as he'd said.

I wrapped my arms around his neck as he gripped my ass, pulling me against his hard cock, and deepened the kiss. I moaned as the low pulse of desire I always felt around him ignited into a fire.

Our tongues rolled, rubbed, and thrust.

God, it had to be illegal for anyone to kiss like this. My nipples puckered to stiff peaks and my core flooded with desire. The constant ache I'd suffered over the week roared into a raging fire.

I needed more, so much more.

As if hearing my thoughts, he rolled his hips, brushing his fabric-covered length up and down my throbbing clit.

I cried out and pulled back.

We both gasped for air.

His face was flushed and lips swollen, my own tingling and wanting more.

Nik slid his hand up along my waist until he reached the lower curve of my breast. "I've waited for you for fifteen years. I'm done waiting. I want you naked. Take off your clothes."

I hesitated for a moment. This wasn't one of my past lovers where we knew the rules. If there was one thing I'd learned over the last week, Nik was in charge, and for some reason I just went along for the ride.

I stepped out of his hold and reached behind me, tugging down my zipper.

Just as I was about to let the dress fall, Nik said, "Stop. Turn around."

I offered him my back.

"I like your hair down. What's the point of long hair, if it's tied up?"

He pulled out the pins holding my hair, letting them drop to the floor, and then gathered the long strands and set them on one shoulder.

In an almost teasing caress, he traced a path from the lower dip of my spine up to my neck, following the trail of my tattoo.

Immediately, goosebumps prickled my skin and my nipples strained harder. His touch was soothing and arousing at the same time.

"Do you know how sexy you are?" He kissed the base of my neck and pushed the shoulders of my long-sleeved dress down, leaving me in only my underwear, thigh-highs, and heels.

"Fuck me." His breath caught, sending a shiver through my body.

He fingered the delicate fabric of my thong before shifting his hands over my stomach and up to cup my lace-covered breasts, molding and pinching the aching mounds. "Did you wear this for me?"

"Yes." I moaned, arching into his touch before letting my head fall back against his shoulder.

He lifted my hand, thumbing my ring before bringing it back until my fingers brushed his lips. He nipped and sucked each tip.

A mewled whimper left my mouth as the sensation caused my pussy to contract and flood with need.

How many nights had I fantasized about him touching me like this? But in those fantasies, I never imagined this type of seduction. Fast, hard, and quenching, yes. But not slow, sensual seduction.

He settled my hands on the back of his head as his palm glided over my abdomen and then down, past the waistband of my panties and through the soaked slit of my pussy lips.

"Hill," I sighed, grabbing hold of his forearm to steady myself as my other hand clutched the hair at his nape.

"Say it again." He grazed my clit.

I gasped. "H-H-Hill."

He circled the bundle of nerves, round and round,

driving up my desire, and just when I thought I would beg him to do more, he plunged two fingers deep inside my core, pumping in and out.

"Oh God. Oh God."

His fingers curled, hitting the sensitive spot only I had ever found.

A moan escaped my lips as my knees bent to move with his rhythm.

"That's it. I want to hear every sound, everything you're feeling. I'm the one person you don't have to hide anything with. I want all of you, Danika."

My legs grew weak and his arm slid around my waist.

"Hill. What are you doing to me?" My voice was hoarse, laced with too much need.

"I'm about to make you come."

My pussy quivered and pulsed as Nik's wicked fingers continued to work the sensitive tissues deep in my soaked channel while his thumb teased my clitoral nub.

"Let go, baby," he coaxed against my ear. "Let go."

As if my body was waiting for his encouragement, everything inside me tightened and a ripple shot through my pussy, convulsing around Nik's pistoning fingers.

I arched up and cried out, rocking against his hand. "Hill, oh God. Hill."

I clenched my eyes tight and let the pleasure wash over me.

I should have known only Nik could make me respond this way.

By the time I came down, a sheen of sweat coated my skin and my mind felt as if it was spinning.

Nik slowly pulled free of my body, bringing his fingers to my lips. "Suck."

I released a breath I hadn't known I was holding and followed his command, tasting my sweet essence.

Never had a lover wanted me to taste myself. I knew I shouldn't keep trying to compare Nik to any of them. He was like no one before him. In a league of his own.

On impulse, I turned, fisting his hair and bringing his mouth to mine. An approving growl reverberated from him as he held me to him and met my demand with his own.

The arousal that had barely calmed flared to life again.

Nik lifted me by my thighs and instinctively I wrapped my legs around his waist, letting my shoes fall to the floor. I scarcely registered us moving until my back hit the soft fabric on a bed. I stared into Nik's dark gaze as he loomed over me.

Being here with him felt right, as if this was where I was supposed to be. The unease from earlier was completely gone. In its place was a craving for so much more. He pulled at something in me I couldn't resist.

God. If I wasn't careful, I knew I could fall for him.

Who was I kidding? It was inevitable.

"What are you thinking?" he asked me.

Reaching up, I traced the stubble on his jaw. "How this feels right. As if this was inevitable."

"I'm glad you've finally caught up." He nuzzled into my hand and kissed my palm before leaning down to capture my lips. "Now, I want to see all of you. Later, I plan to explore all the ink covering this goddess body of yours."

Lifting up slightly, my cheek brushed his, and my lace-covered breast pressed against his chest as I reached behind me to unclasp my bra. Lying back down, I let the straps slide from my shoulders and waited for him to take it off the rest of the way.

"You're a tease, Danika King." Nik gripped the bra, throwing it to the side and revealing my bare breasts.

He cupped one mound, sucking the nipple with his mouth, pulling, tugging, nipping. His lips and hands the only things touching my body.

My fingers threaded his hair and my back bowed as I squeezed my thighs together to ease the need building again in my core.

Nik moved to the other bud, repeating the delicious pleasure. When he'd taken his fill, his lips followed a path going from the valley of my breasts to my belly button. The prickle of his beard was a wicked caress on my delicate skin.

He pressed a kiss to the area above the waistband of my thong and then gripped the sides, pulling the material down and discarding it.

Nik slid off the bed, studying me. The heat in the dark depths of his eyes was molten beyond anything I'd imagined when he looked at me. As was the bulge in his pants. There was no doubt in my mind I'd feel tonight's activities later.

"I've imagined you exactly like this for years. Naked and waiting for me to give you pleasure."

I wasn't sure how to respond. Could I tell him that I'd thought of the same thing?

He saved me from responding as he began to strip, unbuttoning his shirt to reveal his insanely honed upper body. I'd seen the tattoos, but hadn't truly paid attention to the patterns. I'd been too busy handling the effects of being so close to him and wanting to touch him. Now that I was actually looking at them, studying them, I couldn't help but marvel at the beauty of the design. It was as if an artist had spent hours making it perfect for the man in his chair.

That was when I noticed a small section on his chest. I lifted up onto my knees and moved toward him.

He paused. "What?"

"Hill. I don't understand. Why?" I touched the ink mixed in with other designs that spelled my name in Hindi.

He set his hand over mine. "Does it matter?"

I thought for a moment. I wanted to know what made me so important to him that he would have my name permanently mark his skin, but this wasn't the time.

"No. If a man should have any woman's name on his body, it needs to be his wife's."

His stiff stance relaxed and then he fisted my hair, tugging my head back. "Exactly."

He kissed me, not gentle and exploring like before but demanding, all-consuming.

When we broke apart, we were both panting. I held his gaze as I scratched my nails down his chiseled abdomen until I reached his pants. Slowly I worked his clothes from his body, making sure to rub the hard ridge of his cock as I went.

When he was naked before me, all I could do was lick my lips and appreciate the perfection that was Nikhil King. He was truly built like a fighter, someone who had to use his body to make it through his day.

And then there was his cock. Long and thick, standing straight out and weeping with precum.

Without a second thought, I fisted his length, pumping up and down. A guttural moan escaped his mouth, and he threw back his head, eyes closed for a brief moment. I began to sink down to my knees, wanting a taste of him, but he stopped me with a quick grasp of my forearm.

"Right now isn't for this mouth. The first time I come tonight is going to be in your pussy." With gentle pressure between my breasts, he pushed me back. "Lie down. Hands above your head."

I followed his command with my arms in position and watched him. He climbed between my legs, pumping his thick length before reaching to his side for a condom. His cock wept with arousal as he rolled on the protection and I couldn't help but whimper. I needed this man so much that I felt as if I'd go insane.

Heat filled his eyes as he leaned over me and set a palm on either side of my head. I gasped as the soft head of his erection brushed along the seam of my pussy, through my arousal and then out, leaving a wet trail upward.

My heart sped up. This was it.

"I've wanted you for so long. Now you're mine."

His cock worked up and down the length of my sex and I moaned, "Hill," as I arched into his touch.

He clasped his fingers around my wrist and aligned the head of his cock at the entrance of my pussy. "From this moment on, the only man who'll ever know the pleasure of your body is me."

I tried to lift my hips to urge him forward but he barely moved.

"Do you hear me? This cunt belongs to me." He pushed in only slightly and then withdrew.

My arms fought against his hold. I needed to touch him in me.

"Hill, please."

"Answer me first."

"Yes. Dammit. Yes. I belong to you. I've always belonged to you."

Fuck. Why had I said that?

Before I could think about it too long, he slammed in, balls deep.

We both cried out.

Dear God, he was huge.

He stilled and let me get used to him.

"How long has it been?"

"Does it matter?" I stared up at him, too focused on how good he felt inside me.

"No. All that matters is that you're mine now."

He began to move in measured, deliberate strokes designed to make me crazier than I already was. My pussy quivered with arousal, soaking his cock.

He continued the wicked torture, driving me higher and higher but not letting me go over. I closed my eyes, trying to keep how desperate I was inside. That was when he rolled his hips, making me gasp, opening my lids.

He watched me with a smug expression on his face, and I narrowed my gaze. He was doing this on purpose.

"Hill, stop teasing me and let me come. Fuck me like I need you to."

"There she is." He bit my lower lip and rubbed his pelvis against my clit in just the right way. "No holding anything back when we're together. You tell me exactly what you want. Whether it's sex or anything else."

I lifted my head and bit him back, letting my teeth sink in but not break the skin. "Then release my arms and make me come harder than I've ever come before."

A rumble came from deep in his throat and his cock seemed to grow bigger.

He freed my hands and immediately I wrapped my arms around his shoulders and sealed my mouth to his.

His pace shifted from slow and gentle to hard and fast.

I ate at his wicked mouth as I met the demands of each of his thrusts with my hips. My soaked pussy flexed and quivered and then clenched, squeezing his cock tight, tighter than I thought possible. I arched up, breaking the kiss, and cried out.

"Oh God, oh God, Hill."

Thrashing, I clenched my eyes tight and dug my nails into his hard muscles.

I heard Nik hiss as he started to come. Then, his lips found mine again and we lost ourselves in the oblivion of release.

CHAPTER SIXTEEN

NIK

A round three in the morning, after watching Danika sleep for an hour, I contemplated putting my mouth on her beautiful pussy and waking her with an orgasm. I'd had her almost nonstop since right after we'd taken our vows and two days later, it was far from enough.

She'd been out of reach for so long that I never truly believed she'd be mine. Now that she was, I wanted to gorge on her every chance I could get.

What had surprised me most was that Danika hadn't brought up the letters or our agreement even once in the last forty-eight hours. It was as if she was so lost in the haze of lust and sex we'd built up for so many years that she didn't want to climb out.

I knew it would end. Things always ended. Reality would set in and then she would realize she was married.

To me.

Then we'd have to address many things.

Among them the secrets she kept so tight inside. I'd protect her but she had to let me. And that was where we would battle.

What the future had in store for us was up in the air but I knew one thing for sure. It would be impossible to let her walk away again.

She'd burrowed her way into my soul as a kid and never let go.

I wouldn't call it love.

Love was something I couldn't afford in my life. Love made a man vulnerable.

Hell, Kir was a prime example. Without Jayna in his life, he was wandering aimlessly, wrapped in the past and determined to protect Jayna at all costs.

Fuck, who was I kidding? Love or not, I'd done the same thing for Danika.

Something Arin said long ago popped into my mind. *"Nikhil boy, she is better off without you. Get your life in order and then wait. She'll find you again."*

At the time, I'd just discovered where Danika had gone and I was desperate to have her back, hence the reason I'd held on to the chest of letters.

I'd thought Arin was full of shit. Now, it seemed as if the old man knew something I hadn't.

There was now an added problem I hadn't thought through in my drive to marry Danika. The second my relationship with her became public, people would be gunning for her.

She was my weakness. I wouldn't lie to myself and think otherwise.

And my world wasn't one where weakness was acceptable.

And the most dangerous person to Danika was Shah. He tried to control her every move for his benefit. He thought I was the only one who knew the secret that made it essential for him to have Danika's cooperation. With our marriage, he'd have no doubt the house he built on lies was on the verge of collapse.

What would Danika say when she finally sat down to read the copy of her grandmother's will and learned the truth?

Ashok Shah hadn't inherited a dime from his parents. His mother, Sara Shah, had inherited everything after her husband's passing and allowed Ashok to manage the business and finances. Unbeknownst to him, Sara had changed her will to pass all her money, property, and investments to her grandchildren after her daughter had run away to marry Danika's father.

Sara had gone as far as to word her will to include any grandchild, legitimate or illegitimate, making it very clear she suspected her son Ashok had fathered children outside of Jayna.

Sam was the only known heir outside of the girls with claim to the empire but I wouldn't put it past Shah to have strung other poor unsuspecting women along with tales of marriage and a future, only to leave them once he bored of them.

I still hadn't managed to figure out how the bastard had been able to file a will that was a complete forgery. One that gave him complete access to all Shah International funds and properties. But then again, I knew more than most how the right people in the right positions could make things happen and have it appear to be all on the up and up.

Sam insisted he had no desire for what he called blood money, but Jayna and Danika deserved their legacy. Then again, if Danika had her way, she was going to force Sam to take his rightful place on the Shah throne.

Something I had no issue with.

Shah deserved to pay. Not only for what he did to his

eldest child, but for the terror he made his family live through to create the image he projected to the world.

Danika had no idea I knew about the abuse she, Jayna, and Monica Shah had endured.

If it wasn't for Arin, I would have confronted Shah years ago with a pistol to the face. Arin convinced me the best way to avenge Sam, Danika, and Jayna was to take the very thing he loved more than anything.

Arin also gifted me with the one item that I could hold over Shah's head to keep him in control.

A copy of the will.

The very night Shah had taken Danika, Arin and his men had gone in to empty their apartment. As owner of the building, everyone would assume Arin was emptying it for future tenants. When, in fact, he was clearing it before anyone else had the chance to clean it.

Arin and Kris Dayal had had an agreement that if anything happened to Kris, Arin was to take everything from the apartment and hold it for his daughter, including the secrets he discovered inside.

Arin hadn't expected to discover a safe room with a state-of-the-art security system or the lockbox with a copy of Sara Shah's will, Kris Dayal's identification as a CIA agent, and list of people to contact at the CIA in the event of his death.

Arin had very little trust in any government entity and therefore never contacted anyone on the CIA list including Richard Kade, a man he hadn't been surprised to see named.

"Hill," Danika moaned and shifted to lean against me.

God, she had no idea what it was like to hear her call my name without holding back. It was something only we shared.

Fuck, I needed to get a grip.

Her hand draped over my stomach, dangerously close to the cock that was aching to slide into her heat.

"Go back to sleep. I kept you up for the last two nights. You need your rest."

"I think I did my share of keeping you up," she said in a breathy voice as her lashes fluttered open and her gaze focused on me. "What time is it?"

"Four thirty."

She lifted up on her elbows, the bedsheet slipping down to expose the upper curve of her breasts and the thick mass of hair tumbling around her shoulders.

Damn, Danika's breasts were perfect—round, full, and high.

Her makeup-free face made her look so much younger than her twenty-nine years.

"What's keeping you up?"

"You're not going to go see your uncle. I don't want you in any form of debt to him, whether it's fake or not."

Holding the sheet up to her chest, she sat up and cocked a hand on her hip. "Let's get this straight. Me marrying you doesn't mean you get to dictate what I do and don't do."

The hard set of her mouth mixed with the flare of temper in her eyes had my cock hard and ready to fuck this stubborn woman into submission.

"Is that right?"

She lifted her chin. "Yes."

Before she knew it, I gripped her waist and had her in my lap, her legs straddling my thighs. Her naked breasts pressed to my chest, and her slick pussy tucked along the ridge of my rock-hard cock.

"Hill," she yelped and gripped my shoulders. "What the fuck?"

Her outrage would have been more believable if she hadn't squirmed and rolled her clit against me.

I fisted her hair, tugging her head back. "When it comes to your safety, you will listen to me."

"I know how to take care of myself." She held my gaze. "And I know how to handle my uncle."

"He's dangerous. And if he finds out we're married, he's going to lose his shit."

"As we discussed, he isn't going to find out until the right moment." Her hazel gaze stared into my eyes. "What aren't you telling me, Hill? Explain to me, what is it that you get out of this marriage?"

"I get you." I brought her face to mine, kissing her luscious mouth.

When I drew back, she said in a husky voice, "You'd have had me without marriage."

"But this way I get to tell you what to do." I released her hair and gripped her spread thighs, grinding my dick along the seam of her now-soaked pussy lips.

A whimper escaped her mouth and she threw back her head as she rolled her hips.

I almost smiled in victory. I'd gotten my way. I'd do what I needed to do to keep her away from Shah. Even if it meant using her own body and sexual needs to do it.

Cupping one of her full breasts, I took the nipple into my mouth. My tongue circled, flicked, and teased the straining bud of nerves.

Her nails dug into the muscles of my upper arms as she continued to rock against me.

"Hill." My name was a whimpered plea. "I need you in me."

She lifted up on her knees to fist me at the root.

Staying her, I said, "Let me get a condom."

"No. I want it like this. Nothing between us."

God. I'd never gone bare. It wasn't something I'd risk.

This woman tempted me like no other and she was the only woman I'd ever consider raw with.

"And what if you get pregnant? We aren't any way near ready for a kid."

Though the thought of her round with my child wasn't something I was opposed to.

"I'm on the pill." She stroked me from base to tip, rubbing the precum weeping from the head of my cock with the tip of a finger.

I hissed as I grew harder. "Don't you want to know if I'm clean?"

"I already know you're clean."

She couldn't possibly know this. My reputation alone should have made her cautious.

"How?"

"You told me long ago that you'd never go raw with anyone unless you were married."

I stared at her. "You remember that."

"I remember everything."

Then she also remembered that I'd told her I'd marry her one day. I'd said it as if it was inevitable and she should accept it. Asking had been out of the question.

She'd been the only person to see past the hardened kid and to the core of me. She'd claimed me by learning my hopes and dreams outside of the neighborhood, so I was damn well going to claim her.

"I guess that answers my question." I gripped her hips, positioning her cunt over my cock.

"Don't you want to know about me?"

"I already know. Until me, your last lover was that Wall

Street prick. And before him were two others. You don't take your health lightly so I have no doubt you've been tested."

Even though I had no right to get angry, it had pissed me off that any man had touched her. More so now that I'd lost myself in her over and over in the past two days.

"Hill, why?"

Instead of answering and revealing too much, I pulled her down as I thrust up into her heat.

"Oh God." We both groaned.

I held her still, taking in the incredible feel of this woman.

"Hill," she murmured, closing her eyes. "This feels so good."

"Ride me. Ride me until we come so hard that we go cross-eyed."

Leveraging her arms on my shoulders, she rose and then slid down, starting a slow, steady rhythm.

The tight fist of her pussy was a wicked torture and something I'd never stop craving.

Her gorgeous tits bounced with each movement and I couldn't help but feast on them. The toned muscles in her abdomen bunched and released with the undulation of her hips.

"Hill, please." Her nails scored my arms.

"What do you want?"

"More."

"You sure?"

"Yes."

"As you wish." Threading my fingers in her hair, I brought her face to mine. I took her mouth, our tongues dueling and gliding along each other.

As we kissed, I pulled her wrists behind her, binding

them at the hollow of her back, and held her waist with my other hand.

Her pussy immediately flooded my cock and then contracted. I held my breath, not wanting to come before she did.

Spreading her thighs with mine and making it so she had no control, I pumped in and out of her.

Hard, fast, unrelenting.

She moaned and jerked and demanded more as her cunt quickened and then clamped down on my pistoning cock.

"H-H-H-Hilll," she cried out a second before her teeth sank into my lower lip.

The sharp bite of pain had my balls drawing up and pushed me into my own orgasm. I held Danika against me as I shot hot, long spurts of cum deep in her pussy.

Danika's pussy had barely finished milking my cock when her alarm went off.

"I can't move," Danika muttered as she lay on top of me. "I think you really did fuck me cross-eyed."

Rolling us to the side, while making sure not to crush her with my weight, I reached over and canceled the alarm on her phone.

"You have plenty of time to recover before you go to work." I stroked a hand down her sweat-soaked body. "The alarm was set so you would have enough time to drive out to Shah's estate. Since you're not going, we can sleep a while longer."

"I'm still going." She pushed me to the side, dislodging my softening cock.

The evidence of my cum on her thighs had some primitive side of me stirring, and I immediately wanted to fuck her again.

She followed my gaze to my recovering dick.

"Don't get any ideas, caveman." She held out a hand, warning me to stay back. "We have an agreement and I'm going to do my part. That means I have to go grovel at the altar of Uncle Ashok's ego."

"No. We'll find another way in."

"Like hell we will." She jumped off the bed, putting distance between us. "Let's get this straight. I'm going. That's final. This isn't just about what I'm doing for you. I loved Kir too. Jayna needs closure."

My stomach clenched. What was she going to say when she found out Kir was alive? That I kept it from her? Would she stay or walk away again?

Pushing the inevitable back, I asked, "And how are you planning for our affair to start?"

She strolled toward the en suite and then paused, looking over the shoulder with the tigress's head resting there. "There's an art exhibit at the gallery on Wednesday. Jayna always puts the Kings on the guest list. You will attend and hire me to appraise something."

"Am I also expected to spend money at this event, Mrs. King?"

A smile touched her lips, the exact one she got as she went down on me the night before. "Of course. And in return, I'll owe you a sexual favor you can collect at a time of your choosing."

Around nine o'clock, I stared out at the Manhattan skyline and waited for my assistant, Marie, to signal the start of the teleconference with some land scouts in Miami.

The streets below were packed with cars and pedestrians, making me appreciate the short three-floor trek from my home to my office.

Purchasing this property had been a risk, but with its unimpeded views of Central Park from one side and the city landscape from the other, the time and cost were well worth the trouble. Even Arin had had doubts about taking on the project.

Originally condemned and then put through partial renovations for decades, the locals had dubbed the whole block as the money pit.

God, I couldn't count the number of times I'd walked past the building as a kid and wondered who'd be stupid enough to want the ugly-as-hell place.

Sometimes I couldn't help but laugh at the irony of my thoughts.

Now, all of my brothers and I had a place no one could ever take away again.

I picked up my mug of coffee and caught the glint of light reflecting off the ring on my left hand.

Fifteen years ago, if anyone had dared to tell me I'd have amassed a real estate empire worth nearly a billion dollars in assets, I'd have punched them in the face for making stupid predictions that could get my ass killed.

We all dreamed of a life away from the harsh reality of the streets but anyone who said them out loud was viewed as weak. We were expected to accept our lot in life.

Dreamers died.

Arin changed the course of my life, as had the death of my parents, and now Danika had done the same.

I still couldn't believe Danika had just walked out this morning as if I hadn't warned her against going to see Shah.

She was seriously going to give me an ulcer. But I also knew there was no way to cage her. If I tried, I'd be no better than Shah.

My cell rang, making me frown. No one called me on this line unless it was an emergency or they wanted their face punched in. Sam and Rey were expected in the meeting I'd scheduled for the morning so I knew it wasn't them. And Kir had a distinctive ringtone to alert me it was him.

Picking up my phone, I read the caller's name and cursed under my breath. I had a feeling this was coming, but I hadn't expected it to come now, especially when Danika was on her way to Shah's estate.

I sighed and answered, "Can I assume Danika is with Shah?"

"She just walked in."

"What can I do for you, Agent Kade?"

"You hurt her and I will make sure your last words are begging Danika for forgiveness."

I should have been offended by the threat but Rich Kade cared for Danika as if she was his own child. He'd always had a soft spot for Danika, or he wouldn't have gone to the lengths he had to make sure she made it out of her childhood. For that alone, I had to give the former CIA agent respect.

"The last thing I want to do is hurt her."

"Then we're clear."

"I heard the warning the first time you gave it." The warning he'd given to an eleven- year-old street kid who'd found the pretty little girl with her nose in a book completely fascinating. "The only difference is that now I can actually do more than keep the kids on the street from bullying her."

"Good. She's my daughter, even if she doesn't share my

blood. I'm sure you can understand family doesn't always mean DNA."

I thought of my brothers, Kir, Sam, and Rey. I'd take a bullet for any of them. I'd have happily taken Kir's place in that car to spare him the pain he lived in.

"Yeah, I get it." I paused. "You made her happy by being there on Saturday."

"All I care about is that you make her happy and keep her safe."

"That's the plan. Marrying her puts a barrier between her and Shah. Especially with this plan of hers."

"Don't pretend making her your wife was only about shielding her from her uncle. I know what she is to you."

"Then you understand I would take care of her at all costs."

"Make sure you do. I'll be watching."

"I have no doubt."

I hung up the phone and stared out the window.

No one would have believed the crotchety widowed shopkeeper who yelled at all the kids running around the neighborhood was an undercover CIA agent. Then again, who would believe that Ashok Shah's society princess niece was a hacker for hire or married to me.

Sometimes life was a twisted motherfucker.

The intercom buzzed on my desk. "Mr. King. The meeting starts in five minutes."

I moved to my desk and pushed a button. "Thanks, Marie. Logging in."

CHAPTER SEVENTEEN

DANIKA

"Morning, everyone," I called out as I entered through the side door leading into the kitchen of the Shah mansion.

Uncle Ashok's staff moved about preparing his breakfast that had to be served at exactly eight thirty every morning. And Uncle couldn't eat anything simple. It had to be some sort of fancy Gujarati breakfast dish that took at least two hours to prepare.

Kala, the family chef, had her attention fixed on whatever she had cooking on the stove. From the smell of it, I knew it was a spicy mixture of semolina and vegetables.

"Morning, Dani. I'll prepare some food for you to take today. It will be enough for both you and Jayna," she said in Gujarati, the native Indian language spoken by my mother's side of the family.

My father's family spoke Hindi and so I learned both from my family and had a habit of going between English, Gujarati, and Hindi depending on who I was speaking to as a child. Then when I moved in with Uncle Ashok and Aunt

Monica, we exclusively spoke Gujarati, though Hindi came in handy when I watched Bollywood films.

"Is Uncle awake?"

At that moment, Nimesh, the house butler, entered and sighed in relief as if he was worried I wasn't coming.

"Hello, Ms. Dani. Your uncle is waiting for you in his office. You were supposed to park at the front. It's what he expects."

Yes, only servants entered the home from the back and what would anyone think if I was seen going against protocol?

"Let's not disappoint his royal highness."

"We don't want any backlash coming onto your shoulders."

"Thank you, Nimesh. But I'm used to his preferences." I patted his arm and changed the subject. *"I miss seeing everyone. How are you?"*

"We miss you too. And we are doing very well." He set his hand over mine. *"However, it's better for our girl to make her own way in the world. Away from too many watchful eyes. Yes?"*

As the longest of Uncle Ashok's staff, Nimesh was privy to everything that happened under the roof of the estate. His family had moved to America with the hopes of a better life than the one they had in India. Working for Uncle Ashok wasn't a step up, but then again, I was biased.

I smiled, knowing what he meant. *"Some eyes kept us safe."*

"They were more of a warning of when danger was nearby. Just like what will happen if you don't go into your appointment with Sir."

"I hear you."

Turning, I made my way out of the kitchen and down the hallway I'd walked countless times during my teen years. One where I knew if I entered, I'd leave with a list of things I'd have to do to prove I was worthy of Uncle Ashok taking me in.

Today I would do what was needed to get my answers,

including sit through criticism, lectures, and not-so-subtle jabs. I had a plan and I had to get him comfortable.

The one thing I wouldn't do was cower.

Those days were over, and for the last few years, I'd learned the best way to handle Uncle was to stare at him, let him rage, and then manipulate him into doing what I wanted.

I'd lost my cool the other day and that gave him the edge.

Now I had to gain it back.

This wasn't just about the deal I'd made with Nik. It was about Jayna, as I'd told him. She deserved closure. Even if the truth hurt her, at least she would know.

And I had to find out more details on Uncle Ashok's plans to run for office.

I paused for a brief moment at a painting of the Shah family from over forty years ago. My grandfather and grand-mother sat in high-back golden carved chairs with teenaged versions of my mother and uncle standing behind them. My grandfather and uncle looked so serious in their tailored suits, no smiles but oozing status and money. Whereas, my grandmother and mom with relaxed smiles were gorgeous in their heavily embroidered sarees that were the height of fashion of that day.

I always wondered what it would have been like to grow up in that household. I knew it was filled with rules and expectations. But from what I remembered of Mummy's stories, my grandfather, Jiten, was a loving man who made sure his family enjoyed time together.

What could have happened to turn Uncle Ashok into the man he was today? Greed? Power? Probably all of it.

Sighing, I continued toward the office.

My fingers rubbed against the empty spot where my wedding bands had sat for the last few days.

Only a few knew Nik and I were married, and they weren't the type to spread the happy news.

When I'd left Nik's penthouse an hour earlier, Nik hadn't stopped growling or muttering about stubborn women.

I understood his apprehension with my being alone with my uncle, especially after I'd detailed our last encounter.

Nik had to understand marriage was part of our agreement but it would never mean he controlled me.

At least he'd calmed down enough to pull me in for a mind-scrambling kiss as I left.

So far, marriage to Nikhil King wasn't anything I'd expected, but then again, all we'd done for the better part of the last few days was eat, sleep, and fuck.

No, that wasn't true. He'd shown me glimpses of the boy from long ago. The one with dreams and goals. The one who'd talked to me on the steps of Rich's shop.

He'd come so far and had the reputation to go with it. I wasn't stupid enough to believe Nik hadn't engaged in some not so up-and-up things to succeed.

Then again, people like Uncle Ashok acted as if they were above reproach and were probably the dirtiest bastards around, stepping on the backs of the innocent and stealing without a single qualm.

I approached the dark wood doors of Uncle Ashok's office and shook my head as I always did at the size of the structure. To say it was giant was an understatement, two ten-foot by five-foot doors made of solid mahogany. Uncle Ashok had this need to have the biggest, baddest, best of things, and it crossed over the line of gaudy more often than not.

Knocking, I waited for a response and then entered when he called out, pushing open the heavy door.

Uncle Ashok sat in an oversized leather chair behind an equal monstrosity of a desk.

This whole setup screamed little-man syndrome.

"*Sit, Dani,*" he said in Gujarati while keeping his gaze on the papers in his hands.

Once I was in place, he looked up, waiting for me to speak.

Here we go.

"*I apologize, Uncle. I shouldn't have gotten so upset or lost my temper.*"

No, I should have just shot him and saved everyone trouble.

"*It's about time you came to your senses. I raised you better than to act like a spoiled child.*"

"*Yes. Letting my anger get the best of me was uncalled for.*"

"*Does this mean you are going to do your duty by the family?*" He stroked his beard as he studied my clothes.

A momentary frown appeared before it disappeared. He despised my love of new and up- and-coming designers who had a leaning toward casual.

He preferred that his family only wear elite brands that were more fitting for our position in society.

I inhaled, holding his stare. A look that had frightened the fourteen-year-old who'd lost her father only two hours before she was swept into Ashok Shah's world.

"*Yes. I understand what I have to do.*"

"*Just so we're clear. Only sleep with him if it's necessary.*"

We were a bit late for that.

Wait. He wanted me to seduce Nik but not sleep with him. His plan was definitely not thought through.

Instead of expressing my thoughts, I said, "*Understood.*"

"*You'll report to me weekly.*"

"I doubt I'll have anything anytime soon. From what Jayna has told me about Nik, he doesn't trust easily and none of his lovers see anything beyond his bed."

"Yes, I heard he's more of a fuck-them-and-leave-them."

"Yes."

"Then I guess you have your work cut out for you."

"I'll manage."

Discussing Nik as if he were a mark wasn't sitting well with me but I had to do it.

Right now, nothing that had happened over the last few days mattered.

And the possessive, demanding, and equally as giving man I'd discovered under the facade Nik showed the world didn't exist.

I had to pretend he wasn't different with me. That hidden deep under the hardness wasn't the teen boy who'd talk to me about things he wanted out of life that hadn't involved staying in the neighborhood. Things that were only dreams at the time and would have made him look weak to the gang he ran with.

God, I had to get a grip and focus on Uncle and not on how easy it would be to fall for Nik. But then again, I knew if I did, I was setting myself up for heartache.

"You're a possession he wants. I've seen how he watches you, even if you aren't aware of it."

"We were friends as children, nothing more. We've barely spoken since I was a child. Jayna is the one who's closest to him."

Uncle Ashok's frown deepened. He hated whenever anyone mentioned anything about Jayna with Nik or his brothers. He acted as if Jayna never existed, outside of wanting her to show up for social engagements.

He'd disowned Jayna long before she met Kiran.

Jayna had lived through verbal and physical abuse until

she left for college and gained partial access to the financial trust her maternal grandparents had set up in her name. It was as if the second the clock struck midnight on her eighteenth birthday, she packed her bags and left, leaving me as the only minor in the Shah household.

I didn't fault Jayna for doing what she'd done. Plus, it wasn't as if she was rolling in money. Until the age of twenty-one, when she had complete control, the trust only gave her a monthly stipend that covered her college tuition, apartment, essential bills, and food.

"Don't be stupid, Danika." Ashok smacked his desk. *"That street thug has had his eye on you for years. Why do you think I wanted you away from him? My sister sullied herself with a no-named gutter rat. Do you think I was going to allow another member of my family to have the same fate? Over my dead body would King get even a small opportunity to ruin you."*

I clenched my teeth while trying to keep my face emotionless. Papa wasn't a gutter rat. One day I would shove that information down this bastard's throat.

"Then why are you telling me to seduce him? You can't even look at Jayna for touching a King, much less marrying one."

"Don't bring her up again. I've warned you. I let it go the first three times. Until she does right by us, I don't want to hear anything about her."

I almost said, "Go ahead and slap me around like you used to and see what I do to you." But I kept it inside.

Pushing back my anger, I said in an emotionless voice, *"You haven't answered the question, Uncle."*

"Because I have plans. And King and his brothers are in the way."

"What does that mean?" I pretended to fidget with my hands. It was a trait that annoyed him but was a perfect way to distract him.

Yes, it was childish, but what the hell.

"Stop fiddling with your hands. I would have thought you'd have lost that ridiculous habit by now."

"Sorry, Uncle." I laid my palms flat in my lap and looked up. *"You were saying?"*

"You have two months to get me that file. I am no longer going to allow any King to hold anything over my head."

He really expected me to jump at his demands, even without any real information.

"What happens in two months?"

"I announce my candidacy for senate. And you are going to stand by my side as I do it. We are having a gala here, in fact. You will bring King as your date."

Fat chance.

"Are you serious?" The shock on my face wasn't pretend. Hearing him say it just seemed so surreal. He'd never had any interest in politics.

He'd always had a shady politician in his pocket but he'd always referred to them as lapdogs.

"Yes."

All of a sudden, I understood his need to have the will.

Uncle Ashok going into politics meant he had to have everything perfect in his life. And he needed to eliminate any evidence that his wealth wasn't the true hard-earned American dream.

He already had one negative. He was divorced. Now it made sense about his anger at Aunt Monica when she filed dissolution-of-marriage paperwork. The political party he favored made being happily married a requirement. Or pretending to be.

And by marrying Amber Tuttle, he'd wash away the stain of his previous divorce. It wouldn't surprise me if they announced an engagement in the next week or so and then a wedding soon after.

Then there was his rage at Jayna's marriage to Kir and his questionable background. Uncle Ashok was all about pedigree. Kir's death eliminated a major problem. This added to my belief Kir's death was orchestrated as a result of Uncle Ashok's aspirations.

"Is the information in the file that damaging?"

"All you need to know is that I want it destroyed."

"You make it sound so simple. I'm working blind."

"Just get him to fall for you and he will give you anything you want. Have him mail it to me as a gift."

This man was delusional.

"Nik isn't a stupid man. He isn't just going to mail a document he has held over your head in the mail because I'm sleeping with him."

"You will do this, Danika." The vein on his head throbbed, and I knew he was getting ready to lash out.

"What if he made copies or had it digitized?"

"No. He doesn't trust technology or anyone outside his brothers. He wouldn't risk letting anyone get their hands on anything he deems valuable. Besides, the document he has is only valid in the original form."

Oh fuck, he thought Nik had the original.

"Is it something to do with some of your properties? Did you make a deal with the wrong people?"

"You will not question me. Do it or get out."

Ignoring his outburst, I said, *"Let's say I do as you're telling me and step into Nik's world and become his whore to find this information. What am I going to get in return?"*

Surprise flashed in his gaze. *That's right, asshole. I'm not doing this for free.* *"I said I would give you the letters."*

He lifted a brown wooden box from the floor and set it on top of his desk.

My heart jumped and then anger filled every fiber of my being. Taking a deep breath, I used all my willpower to calm my nerves.

"I need something more than the promise you'll give them to me. After all, you made this promise many times before."

"This isn't how it works, Dani. I make the rules."

"No, Uncle. Not anymore. There is something else I want." I hadn't realized until this moment that I deserved to have everything that belonged to Mummy.

"And what would that be?" Rage filled his eyes, and he leaned forward and raised his hand as if he was going to backhand me like he'd done so many times before.

I lifted my chin, daring him.

The second he pulled back, I spoke. *"I want those letters and to take over your place in Shah International when you win."*

"Done." His anger faded and he laughed. *"I was going to give it to you, anyway. You're the only person I trust to follow my directions in running my company."*

I set one hand on his desk and stood, offering him the other.

He took it, shaking. *"Just remember when you take over as CEO, you will cut ties with anything and anyone associated with a King."*

"I expected nothing less."

"You would have made a fine son, Danika."

Fucker, you have a son, and one day I'll make you pay for throwing him away.

"I will also want this in writing. This way no one from the company will think they can plan any takeover. As I'm sure you're aware, a few of them are grumbling about management changes ever since the issues with the zoning problems with the development project."

"I will have it started today. Now tell me how you are going to draw King's interest without making him suspicious."

We took our seats again.

"Since I run Jayna's gallery, I thought an event there would be the perfect opportunity," I started, and gave him my exaggerated details on how I'd play his pawn.

CHAPTER EIGHTEEN

NIK

"How much do you expect me to spend tonight?" I asked into my cell phone as my car approached Jayna's gallery.

"I'll let you decide. But be warned. Once you see this artist's work, you may want every piece on the floor."

"Do I know them?"

"I'm not sure. She has only been in the States for a few years."

"How did you meet?"

"I was island-hopping with a group of friends for Carnival in the Caribbean and we met on one of our stops."

"Which stop? Every island does it differently."

"Umm." I detected a hint of shyness I rarely heard from her, reminding me of the girl from long ago. "It was on our stop in Port of Spain."

Trinidad.

Immediately, I had a vision of Danika playing mas, dressing up in the masquerade costumes worn during Carnival celebrations throughout the Caribbean. I could almost see Danika dancing to the beats and the way her amazing body moved covered in bright colors and jewelry.

I threw my head back against the seat. God, I was hard.

One day I'd show her how the locals in Trinidad did Carnival, and I definitely planned to fuck her while playing mas.

While there I'd also take her to meet my mother's family. I had no doubt they'd love her.

My parents may have left their home country behind, but I'd craved some connection to them, and as soon as I was able, I'd made contact with my family back in Trin. My mother's family had welcomed me in with open arms and requests for forgiveness. My father's family was another matter. They'd acted as if my father had never existed and I was nothing to them.

Their rejection had hurt deeper than I'd expected. However, the connection I'd developed to my mother's side more than made up for the loss. And to this day, it gave me a special bond to my Afro-Trinidadian roots.

"Did you play mas?"

"Of course. My outfit was custom made and absolutely scandalous. I even walked around with five-foot-wide feather wings." She laughed, and I couldn't help but smile.

"And how long did you last with those wings on?"

"A good hour and a half. Then I paid a guy to hold them in his shop for me. Those damn things were heavy as hell."

"One day, we'll go. I'll show you how us Trinis do it," I said, imagining her playing mas again.

"I already know how one Trini-American named Nikhil does it." She emphasized the "it" part, making me smile.

Both of us had our minds on sex.

"That's true." I adjusted my cock to relieve the pressure

in my pants. "Remind me again, what was my payment for tonight's favor?"

"Carte blanche on a sexual act." She answered in almost a purr, causing my dick to grow harder.

"That's right. Whenever, however, and whatever." And I had the urge to collect as soon as I got to the gallery.

"Were those the terms?" she asked, her breath growing heavy. "I'm not sure I agreed to that."

"Remember I always take more than you originally offer."

"Then I guess I have no choice but to pay up."

"I guess you don't." The car pulled to a stop. "Damn. We've arrived. Let me get my body under control and I'll see you inside."

"I'll need a minute myself." Her voice was breathy. "Remember, we're starting our affair tonight."

"Yes, I know."

"Bye."

"Danika."

"Yes?"

"For the record, you're going to sleep with me on our first date." I hung up.

The door to my car opened. After I was sure my cock was under control, I stepped out. Adjusting my suit, I walked toward the gallery. The flash of cameras was something I hadn't expected.

Who was the artist and who were the people in attendance?

The last time I'd come to one of these things, Jayna had brought in a friend of hers from Europe. The artist was some metal sculpturer who had some impressive designs but completely not my taste.

God, I hoped tonight was more up my alley.

I wasn't the high-society art type. I may have the means to purchase the pieces but it didn't mean I wanted to spend my money on it just to say I had it.

"Welcome, sir," a man said as he opened the glass doors of the building. My breath caught as I stepped into the gallery.

It was as if I'd walked into a high-end artist's version of Carnival. But not just any Carnival, it was Trinidad Carnival. From the decor on the ceiling to the style and color of the art on the walls. Then there were the sculptures placed as the focal point of the show.

They were handcrafted, some from wood, some from stone, some from glass. Each piece told a story of life in the Caribbean, and not just any place in the Caribbean, but Trinidad and Tobago.

Jayna had built a reputation for showcasing artists who loved to celebrate their cultures, but I knew this was all Danika.

And this had to have been planned long ago.

I walked up to a sculpture of a boy cradled on his mother's hip and read the artist's name.

Jasmine Dillon.

I'd heard the locals mention her name on my last visit to Port of Spain.

"That's a beautiful piece," a woman with a slight British accent with a hint of the Caribbean said.

"Yes, it is. It seems to tell a story."

"What do you see?"

"Probably a boy who doesn't want to listen to his Mama and she had to pick him up to drag him home."

The woman laughed. "You are very observant. That is exactly what happened. This is my brother and mother. I created it to remember a piece of my childhood with my family."

I offered her my hand. "Nikhil King."

"Jasmine Dillon. You're a bit of a local hero back home."

"I could say the same for you."

"I'm the artist girl no one can make sense of."

"And I'm the lost boy trying to find his roots." The locals had referred to me as the "lost boy" so many times that it had stuck and become a nickname instead of an insult as it originally had come across.

"Because of your generosity, girls like me were able to go into the arts and sciences. Well, more in particular, girls like my sister."

"How so?"

"Your grant to the university funded her computer science scholarship."

"I'm glad I was able to pay it forward."

"May I ask why you specified that program and that the money go predominately to female students?"

At that moment, I saw Danika in my peripheral vision.

"Let's say there was a girl I met as a child who inspired me."

Danika came toward us, looking as if she'd walked off a runway.

My body immediately stirred to life again. God, I couldn't get enough of her, and I'd all but gorged on her for the last few days.

For some reason, I wanted her even more now. This wasn't the femme fatale from the poker night at The Library. Tonight she was elegance, polish, and money. She was making it clear to anyone who looked in her direction that she was expensive, from the black sleeveless gown that was no doubt custom made to the diamonds and sapphires that cascaded down her ears, neck, and wrists.

I couldn't wait to fuck her with nothing on but the jewelry and heels.

The only things missing were the rings I'd given her.

I shouldn't feel so possessive in such a short time, but I couldn't help it. I'd waited for what seemed like forever and now that she was mine, I wanted the world to know it.

Once Shah was taken down, everyone would know she belonged to me.

"Oh, here is someone you should meet." Jasmine moved to the side. "Let me introduce you to tonight's sponsor. This is Danika Dayal."

I took Danika's hand. "I believe I've had an introduction. Hello, Danika."

"Nik." Her fingers tapped my wedding band and she lifted a brow.

I raised my own, relaying that I wasn't going to take my ring off for this charade even if she had to.

"Before I leave you to our guest, Danika—do you have that lipstick I like so much?"

"Yes." Danika opened her other palm, revealing a high-end lipstick tube. "I bought you one while I was out earlier today."

"Thank you. You're the best." Jasmine turned to me. "It was a pleasure meeting you, Mr. King. I hope you enjoy tonight's show."

As Jasmine moved into the crowd, I leaned toward Danika. "You do your business through lipstick tubes?"

Her lips turned up at the corner.

"Among other things."

"What other things?"

"Messy desktops."

"You really aren't going to let me live that down. I like to download documents onto my desktop."

"I know."

"We still haven't discussed this side business of yours."

"It's not a side business. This—" she gestured to the room around us, "—is the side business."

"What you do puts you in danger."

"My existence puts me in danger." She tilted her chin toward a gallery guest in greeting.

"Dammit, Danika. It's not just you in this alone anymore."

She turned to me, the smile from moments earlier gone. "This thing between us has been going on for one week. Marriage or not, I will not put all my eggs in that basket. You and I have a history but that doesn't make up for the fifteen-year gap between. I had that long to figure things out on my own. Alone."

"And what is this revenge plot of yours going to cost you? And I'm not talking about our agreement."

"Nik, he took everything from me and so many others, including you and…" She trailed off and turned, walking away.

What did she mean, me?

I followed after her as she made her way through the crowd. She went in through a set of doors, down a long corridor, and then stopped inside a storage room of sorts, bracing her hands on the wall.

She closed her eyes, dropping her head, and for a brief moment, I was transferred back in time to our old neighborhood, when I'd caught a young Danika hiding in an alleyway after her emotions had gotten too much for her to handle. She'd always been too soft for the people she had to live around.

Even back then, I'd wanted to whisk her away and set her in a place where she didn't have the troubles we all knew. But from everything I knew about Jayna, it wasn't any better on the other side.

She lifted her head as I came closer. "You shouldn't be back here. That isn't part of the plan."

I walked up behind her, pinning her wrists to the wall.

"I'm not letting you run away."

"Nik," she gasped.

"I'm done with you leaving."

She shivered as I grazed my stubble over the skin on her shoulder. "I didn't leave you."

"Get this straight. When it comes to us, there is no more running away. We'll fight. We'll discuss. We'll yell. And we will definitely fuck. But there is no walking away."

"I...I can't tell you all my secrets. That takes time. Besides, are you willing to share yours with me?"

I leaned in, pressing my hard cock to her back. "Every single one. You see, unlike you, I don't pretend to be anything but the man I show the world."

She abruptly turned to face me, her front crushed against mine. "You like to lie to yourself, Nik. I know you."

I gripped her hips, hauling her up so her thighs draped around my waist.

"What do you know?"

"I know what you do for the neighborhood and why everyone is so loyal to you. I know the checks and balances you keep in place so every kid has a place to sleep and those who don't make the choice on their own, not because they didn't have other, safer options."

"Don't make me into a saint. I'm all sinner." I reached under her dress, gripping her underwear and then ripping them from her body.

She cried out from the sting of the fabric snapping against her skin.

"What if someone comes in here?" She clutched my shoulders.

"Is that a protest?"

"No." She reached between us, unbuttoning my jacket and then my pants before working my zipper down and freeing my cock.

"Does this count as our first date?"

She held my gaze as her fingers wrapped around me and pumped up and down. "Not a chance."

"Then you better not run away again."

"I wasn't running away. I just needed a moment to think."

I growled, pulling back, dropping her, and spinning her back around so her face was pressed to the wall again. "Next time, explain it to me. Don't just leave."

Bunching her dress up, I palmed her perfect round ass, loving the feel of the firm muscles under my fingers. "Spread your legs. I'm going to fuck you, right here, right now."

"I'm too short."

"Let me handle the logistics. You just enjoy."

"Oh God. Nik, hurry."

I lifted her knee, setting it on my thigh, and positioned my cock at her slick entrance while my other hand gripped her waist. "This is going to be fast and hard."

"Yes. Whatever. Fuck me already."

I plunged in.

We both groaned.

Danika pushed against the wall as I began to pummel her pussy, meeting each thrust with the rock of her hips.

"Nik, oh Nik. Jay's going to kill us if she ever finds out we did this here."

I continued to pound into her, dropping my face to her neck. "She's going to have to find out sooner or later."

She reached back with a hand and cupped the back of my head, arching. "Oh God, yes. Do that swivel thing. Harder, dammit."

"I will not hurt you. If you want to go there, we'll do it at home when there's no chance of anyone disturbing us."

"Whose home?"

I stopped, pulling out, and gritted my teeth. We were going to have to establish this before anything went further.

She cried out, "No. What are you doing? What happened to hard and fast?"

"You pick." I cupped her soaked pussy, loving the feeling of her dripping arousal and ignoring the need of my screaming cock. "Here or my place? After tonight, there are no separate places."

"Can't we decide after? Right now, I need you to finish what you started." She reached behind her and fisted my cock.

Shifting my hips, I jerked out of her hold. "No. You want my dick, we make this call now."

"Nik, that's manipulation."

"As I said, I'm a sinner, not a saint."

She was quiet for a second. "If I said here, you'd move. You'd leave your giant penthouse with all of its amenities for a place half the size, without the views, without the access to your brothers."

"In a heartbeat." I strummed her clit. "I assume you need your home to run your business, but I don't. I can work from anywhere."

"Turn me around."

"No. Just answer."

She squeezed my cock harder, then worked me from base to tip and back again. "Nik. Please."

"You think this is all about a one-week relationship. It's about more than that. You know it and so do I. To get to know each other now, we have to live together."

"I know."

"Then make your choice."

"Can't we just go between the two?"

"No."

"Enough with the fucking nos," she gritted out. "Fine. We'll live here."

"See." I slid from her grip and angled my erection between her folds, pushing in with one hard thrust. "That wasn't such a complicated decision."

"Shut up and fuck me."

"My pleasure."

There were no more words spoken and only the sounds of sex mixed with our heavy breathing.

When her orgasm erupted, she threw her head back and cried out, "Yes, finally. Oh God, yes. Nik."

Her pussy clenched and flexed, milking my cock until I felt the familiar tightening of my balls. I slid my fingers up her body, cupping her throat and pulling her back. I covered her lips with mine and let go, coming hard and deep in her beautiful spasming pussy.

"I don't think we should ever let Jayna know that we violated her storeroom. She'd probably find some sort of retaliation when we least expect it," Danika whispered through panting breaths.

I reached into my pants pocket, pulling out a handkerchief, and slowly slid out of Danika. Taking the cloth, I placed it between her legs.

"We'll keep it a secret. Though I'm sure Kir fucked her all over this gallery already."

Danika glared over her shoulder and then wrinkled her nose. "Don't put those images in my head."

She wiped my cum from her thighs and straightened her gown. Walking over to a mirror on a wall I hadn't seen earlier, she waved her bracelet against it and the glass popped open, revealing an array of makeup.

"Is this whole place rigged?"

"Yep," she responded as she applied her makeup and then put it back in the compartment.

"How the hell have you gone undetected for so long?"

She caught my gaze in the reflection of the mirror. "Because people only see what they want to see. And sometimes the illusion is more believable than the truth."

I nodded and moved behind her.

"Just so we're clear, this does not count as the payment for my attending tonight."

"I didn't think it would."

"Glad we understand each other." I kissed her shoulder. "Now are you going to explain what you were referring to when you ran away from me?"

Her face fell and she glanced away.

I lifted her chin up again to meet my eyes. "I need to know if it concerns me."

"How did you realize Kir's death was staged by my uncle?"

Fuck. I would have to tell her a half-truth.

"We found a second set of tire tracks at the scene of the accident."

She turned to face me. "You got there before the authorities did. You knew." She paused. "That's the only way you would have known anything was tampered with. The on-scene investigators ruled it a weather-related incident."

My gut clenched as I said, "The exact ruling of the bus crash that killed my parents."

"Not just your parents but Kir's and Rey's parents as well as Sam's mom. She was the target of the accident. Everyone else was collateral damage."

I felt as if I'd been sucker-punched. So many lives had changed because of that simple bus crash on a rainy day. From my research it hadn't even been truly bad weather, merely mild showers.

"What proof do you have?"

"Nik, this isn't the place to discuss it."

"Tell me," I ordered, my emotions too raw to say it gently.

She sighed. "Around the time of the divorce, I was clearing all of Aunt Monica's things out of the master bedroom and found hidden in a group of boxes a payment receipt to the bank account of David Marduk dated almost twenty years ago."

I knew the name. He was the man sent to investigate Kir's accident. The man who conveniently retired a month after filing his report. The man who died of a heart attack while on a vacation in France.

"It's all circumstantial. Nothing to prove anything to the authorities."

"It wouldn't matter. Your uncle has people in place to do his dirty work." I kissed her forehead. "Thank you for telling me."

She cupped my cheeks with her hands. "I'm so sorry my family caused you to lose yours."

"No, Danika, I have a family. We may not share blood

but I have three brothers who would put their lives on the line for me and I had a father who gave me a life better than anything I could have ever imagined. I mourn the parents of my birth, but I can't change what happened."

"You're a good man, Nikhil King."

"No. I'm not. As I said, I'm a sinner, not a saint. I don't mind breaking the rules and I don't pretend to walk the straight and narrow. Are you sure you can handle being married to a man like that?"

Even if she did, I wasn't sure I could handle letting her go.

Who was I kidding? I would never cage her. If she wanted, I'd set her free. But hell if I'd let her know this.

Danika lifted onto tiptoes and brushed her lips against mine. "I can handle anything. Besides, I'm a sinner too, Mr. King. I guess that makes us two of a kind."

CHAPTER NINETEEN

DANIKA

"Are you ready?" Nik asked, taking my arm as we stepped out of his car.

I inhaled deeply and nodded. "Yes."

At night the historic office building Nik owned seemed even more otherworldly, and dressed as we were in our elegant clothes from the gallery show it seemed like we were really in a time warp.

"It's okay if you want to wait for another night."

"No, I'd rather do it now. Plus, it gives the perfect cover for our affair."

He turned me to face him. "This isn't an affair. We're married."

"I know." I shifted and walked toward Lake, who held open the door for us.

When we stepped into the elevator, I felt as if Nik took up nearly all the space.

I studied his face. He watched me with equal curiosity. His beautiful face was set in hard lines and I knew it was because I seemed to do the exact opposite of what he expected.

He shouldn't have been surprised by this. From the time I was a child, I never did what he wanted. Hell, all of our interactions over the years had been out of the ordinary.

"Why are you looking at me like that?"

"You're a very beautiful man?"

He shook his head. "Men aren't beautiful."

"You are."

He crowded me against the cab, caging an arm on either side of my head. "I'm not beautiful. I'm a two-hundred-pound, six-foot-three scary motherfucker."

"With gorgeous dark brown eyes, golden skin that is the perfect combination of his Black and Indian descent, and a body that can move so gently as he makes love that it only gives homage to the control it possesses."

"Don't make me something I'm not."

"Don't make yourself something you're not."

Nik had always made himself the bad guy, the boy who owned the fact he did bad things to get by. And it hadn't changed as a man.

The bad boy had attracted me back in the day and it was even truer today.

My nipples puckered under the fabric of my dress and my core grew slick. I'd had him only a short time ago, and I was ready for more.

"If you keep looking at me like that, I'm going to fuck you. Right here. In this elevator. And the reason we're here will go out the window."

"Why not? I've waited this long. What's another hour or so?"

"Danika," he warned in that tone that went right to my pussy.

I had no idea what came over me and I grabbed him and reversed our positions.

"Fuck. I wasn't expecting that." He groaned. "I forget you're a lot stronger than you appear."

"Shh." I undid his jacket and began to work the buttons of the suit pants.

"What are you…" He trailed off as I cupped his hard cock.

"I want to suck you and then fuck you."

He dropped his head against the wall of the elevator as if in resignation of his fate and I smiled, but my glee evaporated as the cab came to a stop on our floor.

"Shit."

Nik sighed, adjusting himself, and tugged me forward. "You want to suck me and fuck me, I'll let you suck me and fuck me."

We moved into the living room of the penthouse. He threw off his jacket and positioned himself on the oversized couch, legs apart, cock a hard, long bulge along the inseam of his pants.

"Get on your knees."

I heard a faint sound in the distance and asked, "Nik, is someone here?"

There was no way I'd put on a performance for anyone. Then again, Nik would never allow that.

"No. We're alone. I've lived alone for a long time. Well, that is, until recently. Now come over here." He threw a pillow onto the floor between his spread legs.

With a smile on my lips, I held his gaze and lowered to the floor in front of him.

Setting my hands on his thighs, I asked, "Do you want me to touch you or have my hands somewhere else?"

His cock seemed to grow thicker in his pants and I couldn't help the smug expression on my lips. I'd learned over the last few days that Nik liked to take over, and for some reason, it got me hot all over too. More than I ever expected.

I trusted him with my body in a way I never had with any other man.

"Clasp your wrists behind your back."

Instead of following his directions immediately, I lifted my hands to my long hair.

"Let me tie my hair back into a knot."

He grasped my wrists and brought them down and back, settling them on the small of my back. "No. I want it free and ready for me to fist."

Heat flashed in his dark, almost black gaze, making my breath come out in slow, sensual pants.

Nik pulled his necktie free from his collar, reached behind me, and bound my palms together. "You can break free any time; your job is to resist doing it. Do you understand?"

"Yes." I nodded.

The intensity of his gaze told me how my submission to him pleased him. I wanted to give it, craved it. There was a shaking deep in my core, a need I couldn't describe.

With Nik, I was safe. Gentle wasn't in his nature but with me it always came naturally, no matter what he said.

One of Nik's hands clenched at his side as if he was trying to calm himself.

"I want this, Hill. I want you to control it," I assured him and then added, "I won't break."

Leaning in, he brushed a kiss across my lips and then sat back.

Slowly he undid his suit pant buttons and lowered the zipper. Reaching inside, he pulled out his engorged erection.

Precum beaded the tip, and I couldn't help but lick my lips anticipating the taste of him.

Nik groaned. "Is this what you want, baby?"

He pumped up and down his length, letting the arousal build.

Instead of waiting for Nik's permission, I bent forward, taking a swipe of his essence and humming at the salty, sweet taste of him.

I gave him a sheepish grin.

"You like being naughty, Mrs. King." He threaded his fingers through my hair and positioned his cock against my mouth. "Open."

I parted my lips. Slowly, I worked him in measured movements as I got used to his length and girth, going deeper with each downward stroke.

My tongue rubbed the thick vein on the underside of his cock.

I knew this control he was letting me wield was short-lived. He'd take over and move me in exactly the way he wanted.

It was our way, as jacked-up as it sounded.

I took him deep, hitting the back of my throat, and swallowed.

Nik threw back his head and moaned. "Danika."

I lifted up to the tip, letting my tongue circle the engorged bulbous head.

I glanced up through my lashes and couldn't help but be in awe of the gorgeous man in front of me. Eyes clenched tight, face a play of pleasure and control, breath coming out in short pants.

He was a fucking Adonis.

All of a sudden he opened his eyes, and I knew my time in charge was over.

"My turn."

He fisted my hair in a tight, almost painful hold and

began to move me up and down, hitting the back of my throat with every other pass.

I couldn't help but whimper, crossing my legs to ease the arousal coursing through me. My pussy was on fire, dripping with need. If only my hands weren't tied, I could relieve myself.

"God, your mouth. Your fucking mouth. It's incredible." He pumped harder. "Oh, Danika. I'm going to come." Just as the first hot streams of cum erupted from his cock, he ordered, "Take every drop."

I moaned and swallowed, unable to do anything else.

"Fuck, yes." The guttural sounds of his pleasure added to mine. "Like that. Just like that."

I was lost, in the movement, in the feel of his orgasm, in him.

As his cock softened, I released him and rested my cheek against his suit-covered thigh.

"I don't think you have any idea how beautiful you are."

"I'm glad you think so."

"I know so." He tilted my face up, wiping the tears from my cheeks and the remnants of cum from my mouth.

He reached forward, lifting me onto the sofa.

"Now it's your turn."

He tucked himself back into his pants and then pulled the tie free from my wrists, rubbing my arms and drawing the circulation back in place.

Once he was done, he drew me to him, kissing my swollen, sensitive mouth.

I wrapped my arms around his shoulders, deepening the kiss. The fact it didn't bother him that he could taste himself on my lips wasn't lost on me. I'd always believed men never wanted this.

I should know better than to make assumptions, especially when it came to Nikhil King.

"Lean back. I have plans for that gorgeous cunt of yours." Nik shifted us until I was relaxed on the couch cushions. "First, I want to see you in nothing but those jewels. I've fantasized about it all night."

I bit my lip as he slid his palms from my ankles, up my calves, to my knees, gathering the material of my long gown until he had it pulled over my head and on the floor behind me. Goosebumps prickled my skin.

He took me in like a man starved.

"Hill. I can't breathe when you look at me like that."

Spreading my thighs, he asked, "Like what?"

"As if you're going to eat me alive."

He lowered to his knees. "Well that's because I am. I'm about to gorge."

"Oh."

"Any objections?" He rubbed his jaw along the inner curve of one knee.

"N-n-nooo," I stammered. "Go right ahead."

Gliding his face lower, he pressed his nose to my soaked "v."

"Fuck, I love the way you smell. Raw, spiced, intoxicating. Of me."

I wasn't sure how to respond.

He bit my lower lips in light bites and I arched up, one hand landing in his hair and trying to push him to the exact spot I needed him.

"Hands above you, Danika."

"Hill," I whimpered in a halfhearted protest and followed his order.

He spread my pussy lips, revealed my glistening cunt. Leaning in, he licked up, down, and back up again.

"Oh God," I cried out

Circling my clit, he teased the straining bud and then slid lower to plunge his tongue into my weeping core. A lifetime of this glorious pleasure with Nik would never be enough.

He brought me higher and higher, flicking, thrusting, and biting until I was on the edge of going over. Then he pulled back, keeping me from reaching my release.

When my moans turned into mewled cries, he slid a finger inside my pussy and curled it up, hitting the spot to send me into bliss.

I gasped and screamed, "Oh God, oh God, oh God. Hill."

My body bowed and my legs clamped onto his shoulders.

He devoured my pussy, prolonging my orgasm until I thought I'd go insane. Slowly, as I came down, he wiped his mouth on the inside of my leg.

"I need more, Hill." I couldn't care less how desperate I sounded.

"I agree." Nik slid off the sofa, spreading my legs and undoing his pants.

All of a sudden, we heard the chime of the penthouse elevator and froze.

"Nik, I need to talk to you about Dani." Jayna stepped into the penthouse and came to an abrupt stop. "Oh fuck."

CHAPTER TWENTY

NIK

"Hello, Jayna. If you wouldn't mind turning around, I'd appreciate it," I gritted out, trying to rein my lust back and keep Danika from sliding off the sofa and onto the floor.

"If that is who I think it is under you, I deserve an explanation. Now."

"Turn the fuck around, Jay," Danika yelled, causing Jayna to jump and follow directions.

I reached to my side, grabbed Danika's gown, helped her back into it, and then fixed my own clothes.

"Are you dressed?" Jayna asked over her shoulder.

"Yes." I moved to the bar, poured two glasses of whiskey, and brought one to each of the cousins.

My gut said this was going to be an intense and heated discussion.

"How long have you two been together?" Jayna asked me as she took the tumbler from me.

"Not long."

"Are you fucking for the sake of fucking or is it part of a bargain?" There was anger blazing in the amber eyes that were so much like Danika's.

"A bit of both," I answered truthfully.

"What the hell does that mean?"

Danika stepped between Jayna and me. "It means Nik and I are married."

"You're what?" She moved past Danika and shoved me in the chest. "How long have you been married?"

"Not long."

Hurt flashed on Jayna's face as she shifted to look at Danika. "Why didn't you tell me? Hell, we spent the morning preparing for the show together. I get keeping secrets. But not from me."

"You haven't been around, Jay. I spend more time without you than with you."

Her shoulders slumped in resignation then her gaze shifted to me.

"Oh God. Nik, you didn't." Jayna's voice rose. "Please tell me it wasn't a bargain. Not with Dani."

"I wanted this, Jay."

Acting as if Danika hadn't spoken, she stabbed a finger to my chest. "How could you? She's my family. Hell, she's your family. I won't let you use her."

I clenched my jaw. I expected others to think less of me, but not people I considered mine. "Would you rather I made her my whore?"

"I'd rather you just give her whatever she wanted."

"She wants the will, Jayna. Do you want me to hand it over and not protect her?"

"You knew about the will, Jayna? Why didn't you tell me?" Danika whispered.

"What good would it do? It's not the original. Papa thinks it is. That's the leverage we have."

Anger flashed across Danika's face. "You talk about

secrets, but you kept this from me too. Don't you ever play the victim again. I had a right to know. You had your money, I had nothing."

"Nothing? You fucking have more money than all of us. Just because you don't use it doesn't mean it doesn't exist." Jayna turned to me. "For the record, if you didn't sign a prenup, this one over here has a few accounts totaling over a billion dollars in Switzerland."

"And how did I earn that? Tell me. Not because of a nice trust fund in my name to fall back on. Your father stole my inheritance. And I plan to make him pay for it. You may be able to turn a blind eye to his crimes and live your life, but I can't. I am going to make him pay."

"How dare you? He took everything from me!" Jayna screamed and lunged at Danika and I immediately shoved Danika behind me. "I lost my husband because of that man. I lost my child because of a mugging he orchestrated. I fucking lost everything. I want him dead more than anyone."

"Then why did you hide this from me? I deserved to know," Danika shouted from around me.

"Because he always wins." Jayna began to sob, and Danika pushed past me and wrapped her cousin in her arms. "Why does he always win?"

"Not this time," Danika crooned. "Not this time. I'm going to make sure his empire falls for you, for me, for Sam."

My heart broke seeing the love the two shared that was as close as real sisters. It reminded me of what I felt for my brothers.

I walked up behind the women and set a gentle hand on Jayna and leaned down to kiss the back of her head. "Show her, Jayna sweetheart. You know where we keep it."

She hiccupped and nodded.

Ten minutes after Jayna and Danika disappeared down the hallway to my study and the panic room where I kept all the items I wanted secure from the world, I stared out at the night sky knowing nothing would stop Danika from exacting her vengeance on her uncle.

The pain he'd caused Danika was enough reason, but adding in the heartache Jayna lived with only added fuel to the fire.

Some of it a falsity that could be resolved by my idiot brother.

I knew soon the truth would come out and I'd have to pay the piper for my part in the mess.

And here he was, the Ghost of Christmas Past. "You can come out now. Next time fucking close the service elevator shaft."

"Sorry, I wasn't expecting you to bring Danika here." The resignation in his response told me he'd heard the fight between Jayna and Danika.

"It's my penthouse. I can bring my wife here if I want." I continued to stare out at the night. "You need to stop this charade and go live in your place with your wife."

"What did you tell Danika?"

"Nothing. That's just as bad. You've turned me into a liar."

Kir stepped up next to me and leaned against the glass. "It's no different than before."

"Everything is different than before." My gut said when Danika found out, there was a good chance I'd lose her. "I won't let you cost me my relationship."

"You love her."

"I can't afford to love anyone."

What I felt for Danika went beyond love. Her presence was vital.

Even as a girl, she could get me all twisted and following her around, and I wasn't any different as a man. Hell, the woman had me dressing up in a tux for a gallery opening I wouldn't have attended if it was anyone else.

"Bullshit. You've always loved her."

"And what about your wife—do you love her?" I asked, knowing it would get under Kir's skin.

Kir glared at me. "What the fuck do you mean by that? Of course, I do."

"You have a sadistic way of showing it. I know you heard her fall apart. That woman deserves better."

"Don't you think I know this?"

"You know what I fucking mean. She deserves you without your head up your ass. She's going to move on and then you will have to live with it."

"Over my dead body will she move on."

"Then I suggest you get it together. The truth has a habit of coming out, and it seems with my wife around it will be sooner rather than later."

"What's that supposed to mean?"

"Danika is smart, smarter than most people. She picks up on things, and she is going to figure out you're more than her imagination in this building."

"Danika isn't going to figure it out. I'll be careful."

"I'm going to say this only once and it applies to both of our wives."

"What?"

"Hell hath no fury like a woman scorned."

CHAPTER TWENTY-ONE

DANIKA

I bequeath my property, both real and personal and whatever situated as follows to my grandchildren, named or biologically claimant…

My mind drifted to the words of my grandmother's will as I waited for the artifact camera to photograph the piece I was appraising for a new client.

She'd made it very clear she knew of Sam's existence and that she didn't want her son having any control of the company after the eldest grandchild reached twenty-one. Which meant, as the eldest, Sam was the rightful heir of Shah International. Too bad he wanted nothing to do with the company. The one time I'd brought it up to him, he'd given me the death stare and walked away.

The wounds Uncle Ashok had inflicted on Sam and Jayna made me even more determined to bring him down.

"You're concentrating pretty hard. Is there something wrong with the piece?" Nik asked, bringing me back to the present.

"Are you sure you're not bored?" I asked. "You don't

have to stay down here. My place isn't as big as yours, but I have a much better gaming room."

"No, I find this aspect of your work remarkably fascinating. Ten times more than watching you code. In fact—" Nik grabbed my hand and placed it between his legs and over his thick, hard cock.

My body immediately responded and thoughts of my uncle's destruction virtually disappeared. "Not here. I'm working."

Over the last month, Nik had wanted to see how the appraisal aspect of my job worked, but I hadn't had a project come in until this morning. So I thought, why not. The busy season for this part of the job was during the summer and that was also when my new hire, Lilly, would join us.

Nik had watched me code and play hacker and had lost interest faster than a dog who saw a squirrel run past them. The only part of the process he enjoyed was when I'd actually implemented the programs I was hired to run.

I'd felt an easiness with him I hadn't felt with anyone else, not even Jayna.

Nik seemed to find the nerdy aspect of my nature interesting; in fact, it seemed to turn him on and we'd end up fucking more often than not.

I'd never tell him who my clients were or what exactly I was doing, but he just enjoyed being in my lab and watching all the monitors light up with the data transfers. His favorite part was seeing the money come into my accounts.

The one thing I was extra careful of was my Dark Web activities. I rarely went down that rabbit hole unless it was absolutely necessary and after I'd discovered something during my activities working for Solon.

Some secrets never needed to see the light of day, and

with Nik being so close to me, I regretted marking my body with anything that could reveal them.

Though Nik found the ink on my skin fascinating and loved to trace it, he'd only ever asked questions about the tigress, never the tattoo down my spine. It was as if he sensed it was off-limits.

"Then when?" he asked, bringing me back to the present.

"Later." I picked up the sculpture of a swan and set it on a flat plate to measure its weight and let the scanner get a 3D image.

"Did your uncle say anything when you went to the meeting this morning?"

"No. It wasn't anything out of the scope of standard business." I looked up at Nik. "He's making me suspicious. His incessant calls have stopped and he hasn't brought up anything about the announcement or the will."

"I was thinking the same thing. He knows we're living together. It's been all over the tabloids."

The paparazzi seemed to love Nik—well, all of the King brothers and their rags-to-riches stories. It also helped that each of them was drop-dead gorgeous. Someone had taken a snap of Nik and me leaving together after the Jasmine Dillon show and we'd been linked ever since.

I wasn't used to people taking pictures of me or invading my privacy, so it had taken a moment to get used to the attention being linked to Nik brought into my life. Thankfully, Rich had taken it in stride and just added extra security.

"It's not like him to ease up on wanting results," I said.

"Want me to put my men on it?"

"No, I have a few favors of my own to call in. I'll see what I can find out."

Nik reached over and set his fingers over mine. "Don't put yourself in danger."

"Wouldn't what you do be considered putting yourself in danger?"

Earlier in the morning, I'd overheard him negotiating between a known underworld casino boss and a Wall Street broker on a property in the Hamptons. A property Nik would purchase from one party through his company in the Cayman Islands and then sell to the other with money played on the floor of his casino. It was highly illegal and highly suspect and something I couldn't give two shits about. Neither of the parties were involved in drugs, arms, or human trafficking.

Plus, with the security measures I'd implemented throughout all of King Holding, no one would dare fuck with any of the Kings. I'd know about it.

Maybe my moral compass was a little skewed, but then again, I was raised by a man whose compass never existed.

"Point well made, Mrs. King." He shifted in his chair. "Since we're up here, would you take a quick look at something I've had in my possession for a while? I want to make sure it's authentic."

"Why are you only mentioning this now? This lab has been sitting empty for a month." I frowned, looking up from the sculpture I'd just placed under a forensic imaging reader. "Of course I will."

"I had to make sure you would accept a project that wasn't necessarily viewed as a collector's antiquity."

I stood and moved to where Nik sat. "Let's get this straight. What one person considers collector's another will deem junk. It's all individual. Do you see any of the fancy pieces in my apartment?"

I preferred fun pieces I found on my travels, not the

extravagant things most people bought in the majority of the galleries around New York City.

"Since you agreed, let me have Lake bring it over." He pulled out his phone and sent a text. Once he was done, he looked up. "Now on to your fee."

"How about I cook dinner for you tonight? Something special to celebrate Carnival."

"West Indian Day celebration isn't until September. Wouldn't a fee mean I pay you? So that would mean I would be the one to make you dinner."

"First of all, true Carnival is celebrated in February. And second, you know how to cook?"

"As a matter of fact, I do. You want Trini food. I can make you some. One stipulation."

"I'm listening."

"I want you to wear the outfit you wore when you were at Carnival with Devani."

"How did you know Devani was with me?"

He lifted a brow. "You're named the Dynamic Duo for a reason. It was a safe assumption."

"I obviously don't have the wings, but the rest can be arranged."

My phone rang, and glancing at the ID, I groaned. "Let me take this. It's for a project arriving this summer. I shouldn't be long. I had some new pieces come in today, if you want to go look at them. They're downstairs."

"Don't worry, Danika. I'll keep myself busy."

———

I got off the phone and took the stairs to the showroom level of the gallery. Nik was leaning over one of the pieces that had come in, a scroll with a large glass covering. He was sounding out the words and completely engrossed in the poem, nodding and smiling. He reminded me of a scholar translating an ancient language into English.

All of a sudden, I realized he was reading ancient Sanskrit.

I'd known Arin had been a scholar of ancient languages but I never expected for him to have taught any of his sons a dead language, especially boys who were mostly grown. Obviously, I was dead wrong.

If Nik could read Sanskrit, that meant he knew the meaning of the words written down my spine.

That he'd always known my secret.

I slowed my steps. As if sensing me, he looked up, staring at me like a deer caught in headlights.

I moved closer to him and whispered, "You know."

He nodded.

"How long have you known?"

"Since the Little Rabbit came on the scene."

That meant he knew even before there was an us. All these years he kept it a secret.

"Why?"

"Why what?"

"Why didn't you tell me?"

"It's not something I assumed you wanted to talk about."

"You could have used it against me."

"That's true." He moved in my direction until he was close enough to touch me.

"Why didn't you?"

"Because I'm a sinner but not the devil."

He gripped my hip and I set a hand on his chest.

"You married me knowing who I was. Why?"

"Didn't you say that night in The Library that protecting

me was what you always did? Well, I was doing the same. I will always protect you, Danika."

"You didn't have to marry me to do that."

"True. But how could I make sure I could keep you?"

"Nothing can make me stay if I don't want to."

He nodded. "I'd never keep you against your will."

"Then why?"

His words were affecting me in a way that made me want to weep.

"Because as my wife, I could put my whole empire behind me to fight any asshole who dared to come after you. You taunt the most dangerous of people by fucking up their lives, their businesses. You help their enemies take them down."

My heartbeat pounded in my chest.

"What am I to you? Why risk so much for me? Why do you have my name on your skin?" I rubbed the spot on his chest where my name was etched.

He swallowed, the intensity of his dark eyes bringing tears to mine. "You are my everything, Danika. I fell for the girl who saw me as more than the nothing street rat I was and completely lost my heart to the woman she grew into."

I bit my lips, my whole body shaking. What was happening? He couldn't be telling me what I thought he meant.

"Maybe this will help you understand." He handed me a satchel. "Tell me what it's worth, if not everything."

Taking it, I unclasped the metal latch and gasped, unable to stop the flow of tears. Inside lay the copy of the programing book I'd asked Nik to get me the day Papa died, the day Uncle took me, the day I lost Nik.

"You had it all this time."

"It was all I had of us. I wouldn't let anyone have it. I kept it everywhere I went."

I dropped the bag and book on the glass counter and wrapped my arms around him. "Oh Nik. It was always you too."

"I love you, Danika."

I lifted my head and opened my mouth but he placed a finger over my lips. "You don't need to say it. Tell me when this is all over."

I wanted to protest, but he was right. "Okay. Let's close up and go to your place. I want to watch you cook up some Trini food. Maybe you can make me some sorrel to go with it."

"I'll see what I can come up with as long as you're wearing your Carnival costume for inspiration."

CHAPTER TWENTY-TWO

NIK

I frowned as Danika came out of the bedroom. "Why did you change?"

She wore one of my T-shirts and a pair of my lounge pants rolled up at the waist what looked to be about a dozen times.

"I can't spend the whole night wearing a bead-and-feather bikini, no matter how much you like it. I'm not risking Jayna making a visit again."

"I locked the elevator. No one's coming in. I learned my lesson."

"I don't know, sometimes I feel like this place is haunted." She shivered and I had the urge to find Kir and punch his face in.

If it wasn't for his lurking, my wife would feel comfortable walking around naked in our home. Well, one of our homes.

"Why don't you arrange to have the same type of system that you had installed in your building." I offered her my hand and she slid on top of me, straddling my thighs.

"I installed it myself. Do you think I trust anyone to do

that? But if you're offering, I'll take your help with the heavy labor."

It was humbling how she seemed to have completely let her guard down about this particular part of her life. She trusted me to keep her secret. She accepted my protection.

It was as if we'd crossed some uncrossable barrier. But there was another one I wasn't sure I'd ever be able to pass through.

"I'll happily offer my assistance. Then maybe all the assholes in our family will stay the hell out when I want to fuck you."

"There is definitely that advantage, plus the ones that actually matter, like people who want to get back at you for favors they can't pay up on."

"There is that too." I thought for a minute and then said, "I need to ask you something serious. Something important."

She trailed her fingers up and down the skin on the back of my neck. "Of course."

"Is there any way I could convince you to give up the idea of taking your uncle down? I don't trust Shah. My gut says he's planning something. He's been too quiet. It's as if he's left you alone for too long."

"No." The hard set of her jaw told me she was ready to argue. "I read the will with Jayna. Sara *Ma* worded it very carefully and specifically to exclude Uncle Ashok. She didn't want her son to have a single penny. If Uncle Ashok wants to run for senate and keep a pristine reputation to do it, then he will give up control of what he holds most precious."

"What if I asked you to give it up for me?"

Her face dropped.

I knew with everything that had happened today emotions were raw but I had to know if there was even a remote chance she felt what I felt. I'd kept her from repeating my words for a reason. I didn't want to hear them unless she meant them, unless she was as committed as I was.

She'd been untouchable for so long, and then she was mine, and I'd never realized until these last few weeks how I needed the emotional as much as the physical.

Fuck, I sounded like a pussy.

"You'd never ask me to do that."

"What if I did?" I countered. "Would you give it up for me? Am I important enough to you to give up your quest for revenge?"

"Hill, don't do this."

I swallowed and nodded. "I have my answer."

A sound came from behind us and before I could react, Danika grabbed the letter opener on the table behind the sofa and threw it.

"Motherfucker," Kir shouted. "Why the fuck aren't you at Dani's place?"

Danika froze, eyes big, first filled with tears then utter disbelief.

She jumped off me and turned, rushing in the direction of Kir.

I leaped over the coffee table, trying to head her off, but she found Kir leaning against the wall with the handle of the opener sticking out of his arm. He grabbed the hilt and tugged, grunting in pain and dropping the weapon on the floor.

"Oh my God. You're real." She touched Kir's face, tracing the scars and then hugging him.

He groaned and hugged her back. "That's some arm, Dani."

All of a sudden, Danika pulled back, anger on her face.

"How could you? I knew I wasn't crazy." Danika lifted a

fist to punch Kir. "I knew I wasn't seeing a ghost. You fucking bastard."

I caught her wrist mid-throw.

"Let me go, Nik, or you're next." Her anger radiated out of her in waves.

"Not a chance."

She shifted, and I stepped between her and Kir, while still holding her fist.

"I don't think I even know you. The Nik I knew would never do this."

"Danika, please listen. I did it to protect my brother. After the accident, he wasn't well and Shah would have killed—"

"I don't want to hear it." She lifted her hand as she tugged her other free. "You tell me you love me. How can I believe those words mean anything? You told me at the show that you would share all of your secrets. This one was a big one. I can't believe anything you tell me."

She stalked into the bedroom and a few seconds later, she came out wearing her coat.

"You can't leave. Not like this." I stepped in her path.

"Watch me." She tried to move around me, but I blocked her again.

She shoved me, tears streaming down her cheeks. "You wanted me to give up everything for you, but you kept this from me. How is this love?" Then she turned to face Kir. "And you.

You're a fucking coward. Do you have any idea what your death did to Jay? To all of us? God."

She pressed her hands to her face, and I couldn't help but gather her in my arms. She let me hold her for only a few seconds before she struggled free and put space between us.

"We mourned you, Kir. We cried. We fucking still

mourn you. Jay can't move on because she keeps seeing you. Now I fucking know it's because you're alive. I know you've been stalking her. She seems to see you everywhere."

"Are you going to tell her?" Kir asked, revealing more fear in that question than I'd heard in a few words in a long time.

"Dear God, I'm now part of this." She staggered as if she was going to lose her balance, and braced her hand on the wall.

I reached for her, only to have her glare at me.

"You are making me a liar too. I can't tell her. That's your job. Besides, she wouldn't believe me, especially after I just convinced her to go on her first date."

"No!" Kir roared and then winced, clutching the stab wound. "Please Dani, convince her not to go."

"I'm not doing any more of your dirty work than I have to. I'll keep your secret, but until you fix this with Jayna, you're still dead in my book. You're my brother too. Didn't you think I was important enough to tell?"

"It wasn't safe. It was better for me to be dead than alive." There was resignation in Kir's words. "Shah wanted me out of the picture, and he would have taken both of you with me to do it."

She moved toward the elevator, and I stepped in her path. "What about us?"

"What about us? We're married. We have an agreement. I'll get the evidence we need to prove Uncle Ashok was behind Kir's accident—not murder, since he's alive. And I've made sure no one can hack into any of the King holdings anywhere, domestic or international. And you already know the Little Rabbit is vested in your protection. You're good to go. Now all you have to do is back me when I take over the board as we agreed. That is unless you are going to go back on your word."

"I never break my word. If you go through with this, I will do my part." I clenched my jaw. "Dammit, Danika. You know very well that I was talking about *us*."

"There is no *us*. You can't say you love someone, that you'll protect them, you'll share everything with them and hold anything back."

I knew I was being an asshole but she wasn't all innocent. "You want it all from me, but what about me? If I had laid everything bare for you, would you have given up this quest for revenge? I all but showed you my belly and it wasn't good enough."

She remained quiet.

"See. I was right. It's one-sided." I ran a frustrated hand over my head. "It's always been that way with us. I've always felt more, sacrificed more. Every fucking person who saw us together knew you were my weakness. Hell, your uncle knew it when we were kids. Even now, he knows it. I'd fucking give up everything for you, and it kills me to know you wouldn't do it for me."

"Don't you understand? He took my family from me."

"Family doesn't always mean blood, Dani," Kir said from behind us. "Arin taught us that. We've always been your family."

I glanced behind me, telling Kir without words to stay out of it, and then turned back to Danika, whose face was a play of devastation and resignation.

"I wish you could understand. I'm sorry." She moved to the open cab of the elevator and disappeared.

I stared at the closed doors, feeling my world disappear. This time, I knew I couldn't take scraps. I wanted it all or nothing.

"So, let me get this straight—Dani is the Dark Web hacker Little Rabbit?"

I shook my head. "Call Lake to help you fix up your arm. It's only a flesh wound. I don't have time for this."

"Where are you going?"

"To get drunk."

CHAPTER TWENTY-THREE

DANIKA

"Are you going to be okay?" Rich asked me as he walked me up to the door of my apartment.

"Yes. I don't have any other choice."

He studied me. "You didn't have to take a cab. I would have sent a car."

"It was faster." I kept an expressionless face.

As I stepped into my apartment, Rich stayed me with a hand to my arm. "Whatever happened, that boy loves you. He always has."

I closed my eyes, letting the tears spill down my cheeks. "What if he kept something from you, something from people you love, that could make the difference in so many lives?"

"It all depends on if it was a promise he made before you were in the picture. You have to understand, men don't operate the way you want us to. King knows the ways of the streets. His brothers are his blood. If it has to do with them, then rest assured, he will die before betraying them."

"What about me?"

"What about you?"

"Don't I deserve to know his secrets?"

"Does he know yours?"

I nodded.

"Did he discover them or did you tell him?" There was no judgment in the question. Rich knew me better than most people, and I was well aware I kept my secrets tight to the chest.

"He discovered them."

"And he didn't use them as leverage. That alone should tell you something. Sleep on it before you make any life-altering decisions. Much as I hate to admit it, Nikhil King is probably the best thing that's ever happened to you."

Rich closed the door, leaving me alone in my apartment.

I looked around the space seeing different things belonging to Nik all over the place, as well as the lingering scent of his cologne in the air.

How had I gone from a single woman with fantasies of Nikhil King but no plans to act on anything, to married to him and in love with him?

I clutched a hand to my chest, wanting to cry.

I loved him. And I'd never told him.

He wouldn't have believed me anyway.

This whole thing was so fucked up. If only he would understand. I'd worked for so long to set this up. To bring Uncle Ashok to heel.

God, I needed the advice of someone who'd been through this kind of shit.

I couldn't call Aunt Monica. She'd finally gotten a clean break and lived a peaceful life in Miami. She deserved her reprieve.

A thought of the chest of letters from Mummy popped into my mind. I hadn't dared to touch them since the moment Nik had given them to me. I wasn't sure what I was afraid of learning, but I couldn't bring myself to even open the lid of the box.

I took the hallway leading to the guest bedroom where I kept the letters. I picked up the brown wooden chest, setting it on the bed, and climbed on behind it. Tracing the detailed carvings on the outside, I thought of the love Mummy put into carving the designs. She loved art and her specialty was woodwork, a skill considered useless in the family she'd grown up in.

Flipping the latch, I took a deep breath and opened the lid. Inside sat stacks of letters, bundled with ribbon, a gold pendant, and Nik's small carved tiger named Rabbit.

I pulled out the smooth, worn figurine and clutched it to my chest. He'd put his one treasure from his mother with mine.

Oh, Nik.

A sob escaped my lips, and I let all the tears I'd held so tight break free.

"Dani, are you in here?" I woke to the sound of Jayna's voice.

"I'm here," I whispered. "In the guest room."

I wasn't ready for any chipper conversation. I'd spent most of the night reading and rereading dozens of letters, lost in Mummy's words. She'd had so many hopes and dreams for the future, but she'd known from the time she penned her first letter that there'd been a time limit on the things she could do.

For so long, I'd felt as if I'd had no piece of my mother and then she was there, with me.

"Dani, are you okay?" Jayna asked from the doorway.

"I just fell asleep reading Mummy's letters." My throat felt raw, and I knew it was from the tears I'd shed.

"Oh, Dani. You didn't have to do this alone. I would have been here when you opened them." Jayna came up next to me, gathering the stacks of opened letters, then setting them to the side and sliding into bed next to me.

"I know. It was important to do it myself." I tucked my head against Jayna's. "She was so strong, Jay. And went through so much. God, how did your mom stay married to your dad for all those years?"

She shuddered. "I try not to think about it. Mom is happy now, or as happy as she can be. She has her community of friends and her sisters down in Miami. One day I'll get there too."

The weight of knowing Kir was alive sat like a ten-ton brick on my chest. "You're already taking the steps to get your life back. The next can be the gallery."

"It's yours, Dani. It was always yours."

"Umm, no. It's yours."

"Umm, no." She lifted her head. "It's *yours*. It's the front for your operation. I did it for you. I majored in art because it would piss Papa off, not because I wanted to do art. Besides, your shows pull in ten times more money than mine ever did. I'm more of a club business girl. Night and fight."

"Well, fuck. So, does this mean you're signing over the gallery to me?"

"Yep."

"And that means what for you?"

"Expanding my other businesses. I've had contact with a few investors internationally. I'll see where it goes." She sighed. "I have to start fresh, and Kir's memory haunts me here. I'm thinking Miami, near Mom."

Fuck, fuck, fuck. I really wanted to kick both Kir and Nik in the head right now.

"I'll support you, no matter what you decide."

"You always do."

"Well, I guess that means I'm going to have to hire someone to take over the gallery. Any suggestions?"

"As a matter of fact, I do have one."

I sat up and lifted a brow. "I'm listening."

"Jasmine."

I thought for a moment and knew she would be perfect. She was part of the same behind- the-scenes world I was in. She would know how to work the art world and steer the cyber aspects of the business.

"Wait a second, did you already hire her to take over?"

Jayna shrugged. "I merely suggested that she should keep her options open for a position at the gallery. You know she's perfect. Once Lilly comes on in the summer, you'll have two people well versed in both aspects of your business who know how to keep their mouths shut."

All of a sudden a sadness settled in my chest. "You're really setting everything up to leave."

"I need a fresh start. You have Nik now. I love the guys, but they remind me of everything I lost."

Having Nik was questionable, but I'd keep that to myself for now.

"Don't you want any part in taking Uncle down?"

"No, Dani. That's your dream. Going after Papa won't bring back Kir or my baby."

"You have Sam. He's your brother."

"A brother who has his own life. He knows my plan. We talked last night."

I nodded, accepting her decision. "I want you happy again. Living your life on your own terms."

"That's the plan." Jayna jumped up, shoving the covers down and reaching for the box my mother had carved. "Enough about me, what else is in here? Do you mind if I look?"

"Be my guest. I'm so tired. I'm going to try to snooze a little longer."

The clank of things shifting and moving echoed in the room, making me remember how much I hated rooming with Jayna. The one thing she never could be was a quiet roommate.

I turned, glaring at her. "You're making all that noise on purpose."

"Of course, I am." Jayna pulled out a manila envelope that I hadn't seen last night. She gestured with her chin, asking permission to open it.

"Go ahead."

She slowly pulled out the folded document and scanned it. "Oh my God, Danika. Oh, dear God."

I lifted my head, trying to clear my vision and focus on whatever Jayna was waving.

Slowly, a notary symbol came into view, and I bolted up, grabbing the paper from Jayna's hand.

"It's the…the will. The actual will." I looked around me. "The last letter I read before I went to bed, where is it? I didn't understand what she meant. Now it all makes sense. She was telling me about this. I thought she was just giving me advice because it was the last letter before she passed."

I found it sitting on the side table.

"Listen to what she wrote, Jay.

"Hello, my sweet girl,

I see you playing outside. I'm so sorry I can't join you. I'm tired today. I want you to know I didn't leave you. I just needed to rest. Sometimes life doesn't go as planned, but know it can give you other

*beautiful things on the way. For me it was your papa and you. I didn't
need anything else in this life. Don't let past hurts hold you back. You
alone can decide what brings you happiness, and sometimes that
means letting go of what should have been yours for something better.
You and your papa were the better.*

*If you decide you want more, everything you need to take your
future is here.*

I love you, my darling,

Mummy"

By the time I was finished, tears were streaming down
my cheeks, and I realized Jayna was crying too.

"She didn't even have a trust fund to fall back on," Jayna
whispered. "She could have gone after Papa the whole time.
Why didn't she?"

"I don't know. What I do know is that she gave me what
I need to make it right. I'm going to make it right."

"Don't do this for me or Sam. Make it about you."

Why didn't anyone want to make him pay?

"If I don't do anything, Jay, he gets away with it. He gets
a new wife, a political career— he gets everything he ever
wanted."

"Do you really want the company, or is it that you just
don't want him to have it?"

"That's beside the point. He took what should have been
ours. We should have had a choice."

"And they call me the stubborn one." Jayna leaned over
and kissed my head. "Be careful. Whatever you decide,
don't trust him to play fair. It's not his way—never has
been and never will be. And remember, I'm here if you
need me."

"I know."

"I'll go open the gallery. See you later today." She slid off
the bed and left me alone.

I stared at the ceiling for a few moments, clutching the will.

Why did everyone want me to give this up? Why was it so hard for anyone to understand what it meant to me to take back everything Uncle Ashok stole from so many people?

Well, it looked like I was in this alone.

Releasing a deep breath, I rose from the bed, stretched, and went toward my bathroom.

Time to prepare for my meeting with Uncle.

I entered the Andhi New York City a little before ten o'clock ready to set my plan in motion. Everything I'd worked for over the last few years would come to a head today. Uncle's announcement was in two days, and I wanted to make sure everything was in place beforehand.

I might not agree with Nik and Jayna when it came to letting Uncle Ashok fulfill his plans of world domination, but I did accept that he wasn't to be trusted. And that was the reason I was setting everything in motion beforehand. He wanted me by his side. I would have assurances he held up his part of the bargain.

I looked down at my hand. For some reason, I'd put on my wedding rings. I had no idea what the future held for Nik and me, but maybe knowing something outside of my uncle was out there was the anchor I needed.

The lobby of the hotel always took my breath away—it was over-the-top elegance with its high ceilings, chandeliers, and marble. The staff was also top-notch and friendly. Too bad the owner of the hotel chain was an asshole.

I went to the bank of elevators leading to the office section of the building.

"Hello, Ms. Dayal. Head right up. Mr. Shah is waiting for you in his office." The security guard pointed to the open cab to my left.

I stepped inside and readied my nerves.

The doors opened and I walked toward my uncle's office, knocking and then entering.

"Hello, Uncle."

"Take a seat." He kept his gaze on his papers and I held in a sigh.

Uncle Ashok's secretary closed the door and after a few seconds, I asked, "Do you have the paperwork stating I take over your position?"

He looked up, gave me a smirk, and pushed back in his chair. "Do you have what I told you to get?"

"I do."

Surprise flashed across his face.

"Where is it?"

I opened my bag, pulled out a folder, and placed it on his desk. It was a high-resolution image of the will. "This is what you wanted from Nik. Now I want to know. What would you do to keep this from going public? What would you do to keep this from tarnishing your reputation? What would you do to keep from going to jail for fraud?"

"This is a copy. Without the real thing, it's useless."

"Flip the page. You see the picture. I'm holding the original."

"You think you're so clever. Where did you get it? I know King didn't have that."

"And how would you know this?"

His gaze narrowed at me and he gritted his teeth in the way he'd do when he was getting ready to backhand me. "I had the pictures he sent me analyzed after you whored your-self to him. I knew I couldn't risk everything on you following through. Now you answer my question. Where did you get it?"

"In the box you left behind when Papa died. In the box you should have gotten to before a seventeen-year-old boy took it so he would have something of a girl he cared for. You lied to me all these years. You never had Mummy's box. Whatever you possessed was a fake. You knew it, and that's why you never let me have it."

"So you've thrown your lot in with him. I should have known your weak Dayal blood would succumb to the temptation of the streets. You disgust me." His sneer had my temper flaring.

"Tell me, Uncle. What is it that you hate so much, that Mummy turned her back on the money or that Papa was twice the man you ever were without a penny to his name?"

"What do you want, Danika?"

"I want what you stole from my mother. I want what should have been mine. I want this company."

"And if I refuse?"

"I will make all of this public record. Remember this new career, this new love you pretend to have, this new life without Aunt Monica will crumble without your reputation. Remember in politics, perception is reality."

"I see." He rose from his chair, going to a picture in the corner of the room.

He pushed it aside to reveal a safe, opened it, and then pulled out a folder with a flash drive.

"Don't think I haven't noticed the pictures of you and King in the tabloids or how protective you are of him. I should have known sending you in was a big mistake." When he returned, he threw the folder and the flash drive on the desk in front of me. "Look at these and tell me who has the upper hand now. These were captured from a video of a closed-caption surveillance feed. I have the original tucked away for emergency purposes."

I gripped the drive and then opened the folder and felt as if my whole world tilted on its axis.

It was image after image of Kir's accident. It showed the car, mangled and completely crumpled. As I flipped, I saw another car pull up and then Nik came into the frame. He was pulling Kir out, laying him on the ground, and trying to save him. There is panic on his face, utter devastation as if a part of him is dying with Kir. Blood is everywhere. Then a large SUV arrives with a group of men. Nik is pointing, and the men push Kir's car off the cliff before Nik places Kir's body in the back of the SUV and drives off. Then the remaining men stage the area, making it look as if no one but Kir's car had been there.

"You planned for Kir's accident. That is the only way you would have this footage, at this exact spot."

"What I did or didn't do isn't the issue. These images— well, certain ones in the right hands—would make it appear as if Nik murdered his brother and staged it to look as if he spun out on a rainy night."

"You're a fucking monster."

He leaned forward on his desk. "You use the will, I use these."

"I will not let you destroy a good man."

"He's a street peddler, nothing more. Just because he rose in the ranks means nothing."

I jumped up and slammed my fist on the table. "You won't ever talk about my husband like that ever again."

"What did you say?" Uncle Ashok's face turned red. "You married him?"

"Yes, I did. And you can't change it. Unlike Jayna, I have the means to protect my husband."

"We'll see about that."

"You want a war, Uncle? I'll give you a war. Though the one I'll wage isn't one you'll see coming. Go ahead. Have your political career, marry your society widow, keep your fucking company. Just watch out."

I shoved the thumb drive into my bag and picked up the file with the pictures and stalked out of the office, ready to get the hell out of the building as fast as possible.

When Rich saw my face, he said, "Did he do something?"

"He did everything. I've made my choice, Rich. Let's hope it works out." I slid into the car and reached under the seat for the fingerprint compartment.

After verification of my ID, it opened and I pulled out a laptop. Opening it, I took a deep breath, logged in, and prepared to do something I'd never done before—use my alias for personal purposes.

LR: Call for open operation, any takers?

I waited a minute and then a response came in.

V: Taker here.

I had a feeling Devani would be monitoring. I closed my eyes for a brief moment. It looked as if I was going to have to trust another person. This was too important.

LR: Fee requirement?

V: Negotiable based on logistics. LR: Sending over directive now.

I used my normal method of contact when working with Devani to relay what I wanted her to do.

There was a period of silence with no response, which only meant Devani was going to have my ass when we were alone next. Then a message came through.

V: This is doable, fee is your services at a later time of my choosing.

LR: Done.

I logged out and returned my computer to its safe spot.

Closing my eyes, I dropped my head back onto the seat and let a tear spill down my cheek.

"Am I important enough to you to give up your quest for revenge?"

Yes, Nik. You're more important than you will ever know. And I'm about to prove it to you.

CHAPTER TWENTY-FOUR

NIK

"What do you mean she isn't here?" I asked Lake when he said we were driving straight to the event instead of picking up Danika.

Lake shifted his gaze. "Her man, Rich, notified me only moments ago that she found her own transportation to the Shah Estate."

I clenched my jaw.

It had been two fucking weeks since I'd seen her, talked to her, touched her.

She'd all but cut me out of her life.

I felt as if I'd been the one stabbed and was bleeding out slowly.

"Fine. Let's go."

I looked down at my fists. They were raw, and no rounds in the cage or smacking the punching bag could alleviate the pain I felt.

I'd gotten desperate enough to go to The Library hoping to see if the Dynamic Duo showed up, just so I could get a glimpse of her, but she'd disappeared.

Even my security couldn't find her.

Jayna had been seen all over town, and when I'd asked her about Danika, all Jayna said was that she wasn't going to get involved in whatever the issue was between us.

Which meant Danika hadn't told her about Kir and she was going to go through with the plan.

My security would be useless in Shah's place and there was no way I could make sure Danika was safe on that property.

Fuck. What the hell was I going to do?

Whether we were together or not, I wouldn't let anything happen to her.

I closed my eyes and dropped my head back against the headrest.

My phone rang and I pulled it out of my tuxedo pocket.

"Hello."

"Hill."

I squeezed my eyes tighter hearing her say my name. "Danika."

"I had to get to the estate early. I'm sorry I couldn't come with you."

"What are you doing?"

"Finalizing a plan."

"Is it worth it?"

"It's worth everything." My heart fell. "I see."

"No, you don't. Maybe one day you will and forgive me." She hung up.

An hour later, the car pulled up to the opulent Shah mansion. Anyone who looked at the place would assume the residents must have lived a charmed life.

As I made my way inside, I noticed a room dedicated to various press and news outlets. Shah was really going to make a grand spectacle of this whole announcement.

This place felt like a fucking museum. There wasn't an ounce of warmth in the building.

I came to a hallway that I assumed led to the ballroom. Taking it, I paused at a set of doors that drew my curiosity. As I moved closer, I realized it was a library.

Stepping inside, I scanned the rows and rows of books. This had to have been the place where Danika spent much of her time as a resident of the house. I traced a section of books labeled with names of Greek philosophers and then came to a book that didn't fit.

It was a copy of *Pride and Prejudice* by Jane Austen.

I couldn't help but smirk. This had to be the work of Jayna. She'd never had any respect for the order of any system.

A murmured conversation drew my attention, and I moved to a cracked-open door in the back corner of the room.

Devani and Danika leaned against a wall as Danika passed her something, probably another lipstick.

"I should have guessed it was you," Devani said, in a cold, almost icy tone. This was all business. "You've always been too good."

Fuck, Devani knew that Danika was the Little Rabbit. What the hell was Danika up to? No wonder Devani was acting so cold. She was pissed at her best friend.

"There is no such thing as too good." Danika shifted, the back of her slim body coming into view. "Are your people in place to search the office? My uncle has people assigned specifically to watch Nik and me tonight. There is no way I can do it alone."

"Yes. And understood. This isn't my first assignment."

"Do the bosses know you're freelancing?"

"Nope. Are you going to snitch?"

"Nope."

"Good." Devani's expression softened, and she set a hand on Danika's arm. "Dani, are you sure you want me to do this? You've worked so hard to get here."

"Yes. It has to be this way." There was a sadness on Danika's face I hadn't expected.

"Okay, this is the way we'll do it. You will take your position with Nik and then stand by your uncle. After the announcement, you will play happy family. At all times, you and Nik will remain in sight. Jayna is at her club, so she has an alibi. You will slip out at the designated time, and King will remain in the ballroom. My man will meet you in the room. You will have exactly twenty minutes to work your magic before we move in to finish the job."

Everything inside me grew cold. She was going through with her end of the deal.

I wanted to shake her, tell her it didn't matter, that we'd find evidence on Kir's accident another way.

She nodded. "You have to make it very clear that it was me."

"Yes, I know this. As long as you took care of your end of things, I have my end covered. By morning, there will be no physical evidence linking King to anything. And when Shah looks through his hidey holes, all he will find are copies of the files you told me to plant."

What evidence against me? What the hell were they talking about?

I set my hand on the door, pushing it open.

"Am I interrupting something?"

The smug grin on Devani's face told me she'd known I was there the whole time. How the fuck had she known?

"Let me leave you two lovebirds alone."

Devani turned and walked past me, closing the door behind her as she left.

I studied Danika. Her gorgeous face was flawless as always, but her dress was unlike anything I'd ever seen her wear to any of Shah's events. It was silver with a shimmer that made her stand out. And her makeup was heavier than usual, reminding me of the temptress I'd seen the night of the poker game.

I wanted too much to touch her, to kiss her, to taste her.

That was when I realized her gown was one shouldered, revealing the sleeping tigress on her skin.

She followed my gaze and touched her shoulder. "I decided it's time to be myself. Not the girl he wants me to be."

The light in the room reflected off the ring she wore, and my heart clenched.

"You're wearing your ring."

"I am."

"Can I assume you told your uncle that we're married?"

"I did."

"Why?"

"I have my reasons."

"And they are?" I moved closer as she took a step back.

"Would they make a difference?"

"Only if you came to the right conclusion."

I stalked her until her back was pressed to the wall.

"What if, in the end, everything I did was the wrong decision? Would you still love me?"

I caged her with an arm on either side of her head. "I've loved you since the time we were kids and you talked to me as if I was more than a stupid street rat running around harassing the tourists instead of going to school. I made all the wrong decisions and you still saw me. Do you know what that meant to me?"

"Oh, Nik." She cupped my face, kissing me, and then whispered, "I'm sorry I didn't see it sooner."

"And where does that leave us?"

She pulled back. "You'll have to decide."

I wanted to clench my fists. This woman was so fucking frustrating.

"Can't you give me a straight answer?"

As she opened her mouth to answer, the door opened, and Ashok Shah stepped in. "So it's the newly married Mr. and Mrs. King."

CHAPTER TWENTY-FIVE

DANIKA

I stared at my uncle, and all I could think of was seeing his face when he found out what I planned for him. What would come of his threats against the people I loved.

Nik positioned himself in front of me as if to shield me, and my heart clenched. He had no idea what it meant that he wanted to protect me, but tonight was about me protecting him.

"Uncle. Are you ready?" I shifted around Nik as Amber stepped in next to Uncle Ashok. "Hello, Amber."

"Hello, dear. You look lovely."

"She does not. What the hell are you wearing? Do you have any respect for my reputation? How could you cover your body in tattoos?" He stalked toward me and lifted a hand as if he was going to smack me but gained control of himself when he saw Nik ready to intervene.

The anger on my uncle's face surprised Amber, and she pulled back.

Go ahead. Let Amber see who you really are. Let her see how you treat your niece as if she's a sixteen-year-old dumbass and try to control her life. Hell, I'll even play along.

"I'm wearing a dress. You wanted me here. I'm here. I will stand by your side and play happy family but on my terms."

"You look like a whore. I will not have it."

I resisted the urge to flinch. No woman wanted to be called that, especially by someone who raised them. I knew the bastard he was, and it still hurt.

Amber gasped. "Ashok, what is wrong with you? She looks beautiful. She's young. Let her be young."

The vein on Uncle Ashok's forehead throbbed, and I almost laughed. He knew he had to keep everything under control. He needed Amber more than she needed him.

"Amber, stay out of this." Uncle pointed at Nik. "This is your doing?"

"More than likely," Nik responded. "But then again, you're the one who caged the tigress. It's only fitting that she strikes back when she is free."

"You don't want to make an enemy of me, King."

"We've never been anything else, Shah. Now let's get out of here and finish this evening so I can go home with my wife."

Nik offered me his arm, and I slipped mine through it.

"How much of my conversation with Devani did you hear?" I asked Nik as we made our way into the main ballroom.

"Enough to know you're going to break into your uncle's office."

"I keep my promises, Nik."

"So, does that mean you'll need my assistance to stage a coup at the next board meeting?"

"No. I won't need that."

"I see."

"No, you don't. But you will. Just follow my lead for the remainder of the night, and you will see what this is all about."

———

Two hours after Uncle Ashok's grand spectacle of an announcement, I slipped away from Nik in the guise of freshening up in the ladies' room. As I stepped into the women's lounge, a woman dressed in my exact outfit and with similar tattoos on her skin walked past me, nodded in my direction, and left through the open doorway. According to our plan, she would linger in the gardens for the next twenty to thirty minutes, buying me enough time to get back to Nik.

My phone beeped, giving me the all-clear to move.

I walked down the long corridor leading to my uncle's office. Halfway there, I stopped near a broom closet, opened the door, and stepped inside. Along the left wall was a small notch. Pushing my fingers inside, I pulled on a lever, and a slim wall panel opened.

I gasped seeing a gun pointed at me, and then relaxed as I recognized Jacob, one of Devani's team members.

Jacob lowered his weapon and spoke. "Mrs. King. We're ready to escort you to the office."

"Van told you to call me that, didn't she?"

He smiled. "That is your name."

"Yes, it is. I'm a King now. Okay, lead the way."

Jacob guided me through a group of narrow hallways I'd never known existed in all the years I'd lived in the mansion until Devani had given me an original architectural plan of the place. The house was built during prohibition times and these hallways were used as a way to hide alcohol for the then-owners' parties. They had also served as short passageways for servants to get from one end of the house to the other without disturbing the residents.

"Your uncle's office is just behind this wall. I've already inspected the room, and the surveillance is looped according to the specs you gave us. Here's your field kit. I'll wait here and let you know when your time is running out or if I hear anything from the team."

I took the bag from Jacob. "Thank you."

Jacob shifted a wooden beam, and a panel opened up in a far corner of Uncle Ashok's office.

My stomach turned being in the room. I'd had nothing but horrible memories in here.

I scanned the shelves of books that I knew Uncle had never even read and then focused on the portrait of my grandfather that Uncle Ashok kept over the fireplace.

What would he have thought of everything going on?

"I'm sorry, Jiten *Dada*, he deserves what I'm about to do."

Going to my uncle's desk, I sat down and pulled out a pair of gloves from my satchel and slid them on. I opened the drawer containing the three laptops Uncle used for his different business. After I set each of them up, I broke the security on each computer and started coding.

Uncle had threatened the one person who'd always been there for me, even when I hadn't known it. With each stroke of the keys, I embedded code that would run in the background of Uncle's empire, giving me information on every business dealing, every phone call, every step he made.

This, combined with the plans I'd already implemented earlier in the day, would ensure Uncle Ashok would never dare threaten anyone I loved again.

I could have done this years ago. I should have done this years ago. I'd had the means for years.

Why hadn't I?

I had no idea.

Maybe some small part of me had hoped there was something redeemable in the man. After all, he was the only link I had to my mother.

I hoped one day I'd get to use this hack to help Samir take this company. Jayna and I had carved our own paths, and real estate wasn't something either of us wanted. Despite his protests about taking over, Sam, on the other hand, lived and breathed land deals and construction. Besides, our Sara *Ma* had worded her will knowing he existed. Shah International was rightfully his. It was his birthright.

Jayna had been right. I only wanted the company to take it from Uncle Ashok. Revenge wasn't important anymore.

Nik was important.

Now the company would become leverage, not the end game.

"You have ten," Jacob warned as he set a bag near the small access door to sweep the room.

Tilting my chin in acknowledgment, I pulled out a tech kit, opened the bottom of each laptop, and embedded a microchip into the hardware. Once everything was in place, I closed up and returned the computers to their homes in the desk.

"Three minutes. Time to close up." Jacob entered with a group of men and women dressed in black military fatigues.

I took a deep breath and rose from the desk. "Find everything on me or any of the Kings, including Jay. This room has to look as if nothing is out of place. He will know if there is a paper in the wrong spot."

"We know our orders."

243

"I trust you, Jacob."

As I moved past him, he said, "Be careful out there, Dan. It's hard to keep our heads clear when the job is personal."

"Believe me, I know."

I slowly made my way through the maze of passageways and gasped when I found Nik waiting for me in the broom closet.

"What are you doing here? You nearly gave me a heart attack."

"You're not the only one who knows how to sneak around." His intense dark gaze studied me for a few moments before he ran a thumb over my lower lip and asked, "Are you ready to go home? I think we need to have a long talk."

"Soon. But not until we settle this thing with my uncle." I turned, sealing the wall panel to look like its original state.

"Danika."

I touched his lips, hating the resignation I heard in the sound of my name. "It's not what you think."

"What is it, then?"

"Let it play out. Once this party is over, Uncle Ashok isn't going to have any other choice but to leave us alone."

"So there is an us."

I closed my eyes. "I want there to be."

"Whatever you're doing, you don't have to prove anything to me or anyone."

"I do. I need to prove it not just to you but to him."

"What did you do, Danika?" There was worry in the way he asked the question.

My phone beeped, telling me it was time for the confrontation. "You're about to find out, Nik. He's about to find out too."

Nik and I walked onto the terrace of the Shah mansion. He hadn't said a word as we'd made our way from the broom closet, and for that, I was grateful. My emotions were all over the place.

This was it. I'd done my part, and Devani, with the help of her team, was doing hers.

I thought I'd been thorough when I'd searched for details on Kir's accident, and I'd been wrong, so wrong. This time I had help, help that made a living off the details. And since Uncle had shown his hand, I knew what to look for. If there was any trace of evidence linking Nik to Kir's accident, Devani's team would find it and destroy it.

Uncle Ashok and Amber were standing near a fountain when a text came through on his phone. He looked down, and rage washed over his face.

Nik set a hand on my lower back. "Do I need to call backup?"

"Backup is here. All you need to do is enjoy the show."

"Danika," he warned.

"You asked me that night at the fight if there was anything or anyone more important than destroying my uncle."

His fingers flexed on my back. "I did."

"I have an answer." Shifting, I faced him. "You."

"Why me?" The raw emotion in his eyes made everything I'd executed tonight well worth the cost.

"Because it was always you. It took someone trying to hurt you for me to see it."

Uncle Ashok stalked toward me before Nik could respond, grabbing my arm and hurling me forward and away from Nik. "What have you done?"

Nik grabbed my uncle by the throat. "Let her go, or I will break your neck, and I don't care how many cameras are here."

Uncle Ashok released my arm, and it took all my strength not to rub at the spot where I knew bruises would appear. I wouldn't give him the satisfaction of knowing he'd hurt me.

Instead, I blew off the hair that flew into my face and said, "You threatened me and everyone I love. I just insured you can't hurt us anymore."

"What did you do, Danika?" Nik whispered as he came to my side.

I stared at my uncle. "I bought out all of his outstanding debts, business and personal, with a subsidiary I created under King Holding. My uncle has overextended himself and was on the verge of putting Shah International into bankruptcy."

If it hadn't been for a tip from Devani, I wouldn't have known about the loans he'd taken out after the zoning issues he'd dealt with a few months back. It had given me the perfect opportunity to use the money I'd accrued over the last few years. Buying the debt under one of the King Holding shell companies had been the most challenging part of the whole deal, but after a few favors and a little assistance from Jayna as a signer for the company, everything came together.

"Where did you get that kind of capital? There is no way King has that amount of cash lying around to broker a deal of that magnitude in a matter of hours."

I continued to hold Uncle Ashok's gaze, even as I felt the weight of Nik's on me. "Let's say King Holding has an angel investor. Someone with deep pockets. Someone who is vested in the company's success."

Uncle Ashok shrugged. "Don't think for one second this

makes any difference in my world. As long as I pay on time, you can't do anything to me. And remember, I still have the photographs and the recordings."

"What photographs and recordings?" Nik asked.

"Didn't your wife tell you? I have you on surveillance, moving your brother's body. In the right hands, the information could implicate you in Kiran King's death." The smugness on Uncle Ashok's face made me want to slap him.

"We both know the truth. I had nothing to do with the wreck. You caused it." Nik set a hand on my hip. "As you caused the bus crash that killed my parents."

"Prove it." Uncle Ashok looked toward Amber and then back at Nik and me.

The poor woman finally saw the real Ashok Shah.

"That's right," my uncle continued. "You can't. I'm the only one with evidence to convict anyone of murder. You want to keep your husband safe, then you better fall in line, little girl."

"Uncle, you think you hold all the cards, but you don't. You want to play the blackmail game. Let's play, but it will be on my terms."

"Meaning?"

"Meaning exactly this: if you ever threaten my family or me ever again, I will shred your reputation. Isn't that what you value? Your image. Your political career hinges on it. I don't need to give you the details. Just know I have multiple means to do it."

"You think you're so clever."

"She is clever. She maneuvered this, under your nose." Nik took my hand, pulling me away from my uncle, and then muttered, "And mine."

CHAPTER TWENTY-SIX

NIK

My emotions roiled in my chest as I led Danika out of the Shah mansion. As we slid into the limo, neither of us said anything. We only stared at each other.

I tried to wrap my mind around what had just happened.

The secrecy about tonight, the conversation with Devani, the disappearance from the event finally made sense.

She'd turned vigilante.

For me.

To protect me.

She could have used the will, but she'd given me the means of making sure Shah could never reveal the photos or recording without it becoming a detriment to him. But then again, there wouldn't be any evidence showing I was anywhere near Kir's accident.

What had it cost her to make this happen?

After about fifteen minutes, I asked, "Why?"

She'd given up the one thing she wanted more than anything. I had to know why. I couldn't hope. Hope wasn't something men like me could take lightly. Plus, I needed a goddammed straight answer from her.

She looked up through her long lashes. "You know why."

"Say it."

She shifted, setting her hands in her lap as tears filled her eyes. "You're more important than him...than my revenge... than anything. I would protect you at all costs. I know that now."

My heart hammered in my chest and my hands shook as I reached for her and drew her onto my lap.

"Say it, Danika."

"Say what?" Her palms settled on my chest.

"Tell me why." I tilted her chin up with a finger.

She cupped my face in both of her hands and leaned in. "Because I love you. I've always loved you."

I pressed my lips to her forehead and then her mouth. "I never thought I'd hear those words."

We kissed as I laid her back against the seat. It had been two weeks since I'd last touched her but it felt as if it had been years. I needed her like a man starved.

As if she felt the same desperation, we both began to tear at the other's clothes, desperate to remove anything that separated us from touching hot skin.

"Nik, hurry. I need you in me."

"Knees on the floor, ass in the air, hand against the seat."

Without hesitation, she positioned herself and then looked over her shoulder and lifted her brow. "I'm waiting."

I laughed for the first time in two weeks and climbed in behind her, sliding my fingers between her folds and into her cunt.

Danika pushed back. "Oh God. Yes."

Pumping in and out, I asked, "Want my fingers or cock?"

"Cock, definitely cock. Nothing like your cock. Give me your cock."

Pulling out, I brought my fingers to her lips.

Without saying anything, she sucked, licking her essence clean, and then lifted her face for a kiss. I sealed my lips across hers, drowning in her heady flavor.

This woman was mine, finally, truly mine.

The world finally knew it. No more hiding it. She'd claimed me as much as I'd claimed her.

Breaking our kiss, I pressed her forward with a hand to her lower back and used my knees to widen her stance.

"Are you ready for me?"

"Yes," she gasped. "More than ready."

I took hold of my cock and ran it up and down the seam of her soaked cunt, eliciting a moan from her as her fingernails scored the leather of the seat.

A second later, I drove home into her beautiful pussy.

"Nik," Danika cried out.

"That's it, baby. I want to hear how good it is."

"It's always good with you. It's fucking incredible."

I drove into her and she rode each thrust.

"I love you, Danika."

"I love you, Hill."

There were no more words, just the sounds of our bodies, and when we came it was in a loud chorus of cries and moans with the thump of the road underneath us.

"I need you to do something for me," Danika said to me a few hours later as we lay in bed.

"What?"

"Tell Kir that it's time to come clean with Jayna or risk losing her forever."

I knew she was right.

"I'll do my best. He's stubborn as hell."

"She's ready to move on."

I knew the day would come. Jayna was a beautiful woman; she couldn't live the life of a window indefinitely.

"I hear you." I ran a hand over her knuckles and smiled. "So, you ever going to forgive Kir for scaring you?"

"I forgave him for that almost immediately. Forgiving him for what he is putting Jayna through is another thing. I'm part of the problem now."

"I'm sorry you're in the middle of this." I pulled her against me.

"He has to do something soon or she's going to leave and I'm going to help her start a new life."

I stiffened. "Danika."

"No, Nik. No more hiding. Some secrets I'll keep but not this one, not from Jayna. He mans up or loses her forever."

"Understood."

After a few moments of silence, Danika lifted her head from my chest. "I have a favor to ask you."

"Is that right?"

"Yes."

"You do know my favors come at a price."

She rose, letting the sheet slip and revealing her naked body as she straddled my hips. "I'm sure that what I have to offer you is more than enough compensation."

"Mrs. King, I'll take what you have to offer and expect even more. Are you willing to risk it?"

She wrapped her arms around my neck. "Absolutely. I'll risk everything."

Continue with the next book in the Street Kings Series now
– *Vicious Prince*

Or

Start a new series while you wait – *Master of Sin*

<<<<>>>>

READ THE NEXT BOOK IN THE STREET KINGS SERIES

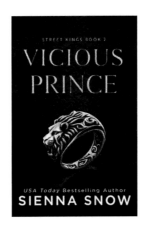

I'm not a good man.
I'm the darkness, the danger, the enforcer behind the empire.
No one sees me unless I want them to.
Then one day, she found me, showing me a life beyond the shadows of the streets. Until one wrong turn and our fairy-tale shattered, leaving me back in darkness. In a place I can only reach her by destroying her world.
So, I wait.

But waiting isn't something she is willing to do. She's forging a new life without me, in the path of our enemies.

Now the monster in me is forced out of the shadows, ready to fight for what belongs to me. She will learn that protecting her is my mission and a life without me isn't an option.

READ THE FIRST BOOK IN THE GODS OF VEGAS SERIES

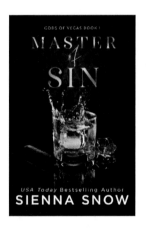

It was always him...

The one I shouldn't want, shouldn't crave, the one who could destroy my carefully built life.

Hagen Lykaios was the essence of sin, indulgence, and danger - everything I knew to avoid.

All it took was one unexpected touch, and he consumed me, left me begging, needy, and hungry for more.

He said if I entered his world he would corrupt me, own me, and change all that I had ever known...and you know what? ***I went anyway.***

BOOKS BY SIENNA SNOW

Rules of Engagement

Rule Breaker

Rule Master

Rule Changer

Politics of Love

Celebrity

Senator

Commander

Gods of Vegas

Master of Sin

Master of Games

Master of Revenge

Master of Secrets

Master of Control

Master of Fortune

Sweetest Sin

Intrigued By Love

Hidden Truths (HEA Collective Exclusive)

Street Kings

Dangerous King

Vicious Prince

Deceptive Knight

Ruthless Heir

Collections

Reckless Rome (A Cocky Hero Club Novel)

Take Me To Bed (Limited Anthology - 2019)

Meet Me Under The Mistletoe (Limited Anthology - 2021)

Nightingale (Charity anthology supporting Ukraine - April 2022)

Darkly Ever After (Organized Crime Anthology – April 2022)

ABOUT THE AUTHOR

Inspired by her years working in corporate America, Sienna loves to serve up stories woven around confident and successful women who know what they want and how to get it, both in – and out – of the bedroom.

Her heroines are fresh, well-educated, and often find love and romance through atypical circumstances. Sienna treats her readers to enticing slices of hot romance infused with empowerment and indulgent satisfaction.

Sienna loves the life of travel and adventure. She plans to visit even the farthest corners of the world and delight in experiencing the variety of cultures along the way. When she isn't writing or traveling, Sienna is working on her "happily ever after" with her husband and children.

Sign up for her newsletter to be notified of releases, book sales, events and so much more. http://www.siennasnow.com/newsletter

contact@siennasnow.com